To The Heart of The Man

Belinda Tobin

To The Heart of The Man

Published by Bel House Books

Paperback ISBN: 978-1-7637246-5-5

EBook ISBN: 978-1-7637246-6-2

For permissions or enquiries, please contact:

Bel House Books

Email: bhb@heart-led.pub

Website: www. heart-led.pub/bel-house-books

First Edition: October 2024

A catalogue record for this book is available from the National Library of Australia

Other titles from Bel House Books:

I'm Sorry Juno

The Love Life of a Chameleon

The Emptiness Algorithm

Crucifixus

I acknowledge the Yuggera and Ugarapul peoples as the Traditional Owners of the lands and waterways where this book was written. I honour the wisdom that lives within the cultures of our First Nations peoples and celebrate its continuity. I pay my deep respects to Elders past, present and future and send my greatest gratitude for all they do for the life of this land.

Always was, always will be.

To Aunty Fay, whose research into our family's history has not only preserved our past but also shaped my understanding of who I am. You are the inspiration behind every page.

This novel is inspired by real historical events and figures. While every effort has been made to remain true to the known facts, certain details, characters, and events have been artistically embellished or imagined by the author to enrich the narrative.

"No man's life can be encompassed in one telling.

There is no way to give each year its allotted weight, to include each event, each person who helped to shape a lifetime.

What can be done is to be faithful in spirit to the record and to try to find one's way to the heart of the man."

Richard Attenborough

Eighteenth century oil painting of the convict vessel The Pitt.

16 July 1791

The Pitt stands ready, poised for departure come the morrow's light. Today, I bore witness to the harrowing sight of four hundred and forty three souls, men and women both shackled and herded below decks like livestock bound for market. Their quarters, a cramped hell below the waterline, overflowed with the stench of despair and confinement. In their cursory inspection, the navy deemed fit to remove but thirty-three of these unfortunate souls, citing overcrowding. Yet, even with this meagre reduction, the ship remained perilously burdened, her holds crammed with casks and cases, leaving scarce room for air or comfort.

My berth in the Great Cabin shared with my chest of belongings, offers a solitary refuge amidst the storm of activity. I share the space with my fellow officers, a motley crew of the NSW Corps. Some are men of integrity, with impeccable manners, while others are simple, purely uncivilised and underhanded. This mix is but a mirror to the fractured society from which we are dispatched.

The sun cast a warm, golden glow over the sea but did little to ease my distress. The hot air was thick, not just with brine, but with the stench of human misery. The confined space below decks reeked of unwashed bodies, illness, and the faint, lingering odour of fear; I know it well. I feel it, too.

For in addition to the bodies and basic supplies, our ship is also laden with munitions. The French fleet are fierce. They are a mighty enemy and have a resolve for revolution that may test our very existence. We may be called to stand in defence of our kingdom and, by my oath, to offer my life on the Major's orders.

The din of the day has also left a lasting echo in my ears—a cacophony of angry orders, clanking chains, despairing cries, and the incessant shouting and swearing of the sailors. The virtuous amongst us watched on uncomfortably. While those with the wicked hearts began a wager on how many this voyage would doom to the depths, and claimed the women they would have when the Major was not looking.

It was sheer cruelty to command the convicts to cast their eyes downward, for we all knew full well that for many, this may be the last sky they will ever see.

However, amid this tumult, if I am to be honest, I also felt a spark of excitement, a fervour for the journey ahead. The past three months have been a tempest of preparation. Under Uncle John's tutelage, I have matured, stepping beyond the threshold of my eighteenth year into the realm of manhood. Now I have the chance to embark upon a true adventure across the seas and to an unknown land. I do so, mindful of the duty I carry to make my family proud, and I am committed to this endeavour.

Although this resolve brings little ease to the pain of parting from my family. We are all still grieving the loss of Thomas, my older brother and my best friend. He was the one who bore the burdens of our family and eased my fears. After Father died, Thomas took the place of responsibility and reliability. I was allowed to remain free, to entertain and engage with the patrons and to spend time with my pony. Thomas, with his firm but fair hand, ensured that our Inn, the Red Lion was a safe place and one of respect. I was tasked with ensuring it was also a place of entertainment and ease, and so I spent time with the patrons, joking and jesting, serving and dancing. Between us both, Thomas and I, we made our Inn a place of respectful if not sometimes raucous, pleasure.

My heart aches for my mother and five sisters, now tasked with the upkeep of the Inn and supported only by my little brother Hugh, still a boy and not yet a man. The future marriages of my sisters are a matter of great import and weighs heavily on my mind. I trust, though, wholeheartedly, in my mother's wisdom to guide them to men of valour and virtue, shielding them from the scoundrels that seek to frequent our doorstep. My mother and sisters are strong women, and will do what is right. I only worry about the men that may enter their lives and the legacy they may leave.

I do envy my little brother, Hugh, now ten, who receives the constant adoration of his older sisters. While I am privileged to be in this position and greatly appreciative of the adventure ahead, I can also attest to my heart, wishing deeply that I was back amongst the sympathies and sensibilities of my sisters and being a big brother to Hugh. I would love nothing more than to be for him what Thomas was for me. Maybe one day I will have the chance if he, too, comes to the colony.

I cannot think of my sisters without my mind inevitably drifting to the women consigned to the gun decks, cowering and crushed. Some are no older than my dear sister Sarah, now in her fifteenth year. Their youth is now surely snuffed out by the harsh reality of their circumstances. Their beauty is buried deep beneath the dirt and disease of prison life. I am sure even the Lord would not prescribe such a punishment so tortuous for crimes so petty. I find it so difficult to reconcile their treatment with the notion of justice.

I am resolved to extend whatever measure of care and prayer I can muster for these souls. My time at the Inn, amidst the transient fortunes of our patrons, has taught me the fragile nature of freedom. A few evil events can turn a man from a wealthy merchant to a miser. Many loyal customers, whom I once helped ease their minds with merriment, now find themselves ensnared in the merciless grip of the law, their fates sealed and dispatched to floating purgatories. I know how quickly the winds of fortune can change, and I will extend compassion to those below while praying that with God's grace, I will avoid the same path.

My heart is mildly eased by Major Grose, our commander, a man of military experience and apparent fairness. Twice wounded in the American Revolutionary War, he has seen several battles, and I believe him to be brave.

Nevertheless, looking at the state of this ship, its cargo and crew, he will need all the courage that his heart and mind can muster. His family's presence is a grounding anchor amidst the uncertain tides ahead, instilling a measure of hope. At least while the Major's wife and children walk the decks, the crudest of man's behaviour may be curbed.

In silent prayer, I beseech the Lord's protection over us as we navigate our unknown fate. And may He shelter and sustain my family, keeping their bodies in health and hearts in peace.

TO THE HEART OF THE MAN

13 February 1792

Preparations are underway for our arrival at Port Jackson tomorrow. The relief is so great that I fear I may collapse when I take my first steps in my new country. It has been a journey of seven months—a span of time filled with trials that have tested the very limits of my endurance and faith. There were times when I was tempted to throw myself at the mercy of the sea, firm in the belief that it would offer more compassion than this ship and my comrades.

Throughout this voyage, I found myself unable to pen my thoughts, afraid that acknowledging the horrors we faced would cement them into reality, dragging me further into despair. The daily disturbances of shipboard life also left little room for reflection, and I feared my writings might be seen as a neglect of duties. My prayers were a far more productive use of my time and could be done without risking the criticism of the uncivilised rabble.

The first week, we encountered mild weather and were able to establish a routine. I took particular pleasure in those moments spared, aiding and entertaining Major Grose's children. They, like so many others, suffered from severe seasickness. Still, we were able to restore their vitality within a few days. Such compassion was not to be shown towards the convicts, being reminded by the Major that they were prisoners, not people. And yet some of the convicts showed that they have even greater resilience and respect than many of our own men.

Once they had recovered, the children's laughter provided a stark contrast to the hardship of those below their little feet. Their innocence reminded me of the purity and hope that children represent. Truly, they are God's creatures, and in their eyes, I see a future I yearn to be a part of. I often dream of the day when I will be blessed with many children of my own, to nurture them and witness their unfettered joy and discovery of this new world.

Our routine was shocked and shattered when smallpox broke out, turning the Pitt into a floating infirmary. Dr Jameson's supply of cowpox scabs, meant as a preventative, had deteriorated and failed to offer protection. By the time we anchored at St Jago, many convicts were in agony, and the crew was alarmed. Before we weighed anchor, we had consigned fifteen souls to the sea, wrapped in sailcloth, and sent off with prayers. I had seen dead bodies before, but none had filled me with such dread. I could not help but see my future in those shrouded figures.

As the outbreak waned, the heat rose to levels that had me believing we had descended into hell itself. I had never before imagined that God would inflict such intensity. The ship became a refuge for vermin fleeing the scorching heat. Our days were spent battling bugs, beetles, mice, rats, and the extremity of the elements. We were either wetting the timber to prevent it from drying out or drying ourselves after the tempestuous rains that threatened to engulf us. This world seemed far removed from the divine creation I had once envisioned, revealing instead a realm of merciless wildness.

The doldrums brought calm to the waters but not in our hearts. It was deceptive, a stillness not of peace but of foreboding. We all knew the lack of wind would mean an extension of our journey, and this prospect caused much despair. The appearance of scurvy among the convicts marked yet another trial; their bodies turned into tapestries of blisters and ulcers. My stomach cramped with every inspection, with the stench of decay so intense I began to believe this a fate worse than death. The punishment that these people would face on land seemed trivial compared to the torture of this voyage.

A fever among the crew and their families followed, sparing the convicts but decimating our ranks. Quarantine measures isolated the afflicted, leaving many to face their end in solitude or alongside their equally stricken kin. I could not be there to care for my comrades, only able to offer condolences to any family left behind. There were no cries for the convicts who were cast into the sea. The crew did not believe the prisoners deserved their sorrow. Yet the outpouring of grief for the fallen officers and their families was full and forceful. Because each death of a comrade came with the realisation that God did not care for rank.

By Rio de Janeiro, we had lost another thirty-two souls, each being dispatched with a prayer for their peace in the afterlife. It was there, near Rio, that Dr. Jameson's urging granted us a week's respite on an island—a brief sanctuary where the natural beauty seemed almost surreal. The island, a paradise untouched, boasted waters so clear they seemed more air than liquid and sands so pristine they sparkled under the sun's embrace. This unexpected haven offered us a momentary escape from the grim reality aboard The Pitt. Fresh food, cool water swims, and the sheer tranquillity of our surroundings were a balm to our beleaguered spirits. The vibrancy of life on the island, from the lush foliage to the exotic calls of unseen creatures, was a stark contrast to the death and despair we had become accustomed to. For a fleeting week, we indulged in the grace of God's creation, a world away from the fear that had seeped into every crevice of our ship.

Upon our return, our senses were again met with the sights, sounds and smells of sickness, excrement and death. The odours had been masked only slightly with lime and gunpowder, but to the nostrils that had a week of nothing but fresh air, it was a ghastly onslaught. I realised how acclimatised one can become to horrific conditions. Four convicts had escaped, and in truth, I was envious of their ability to stay on this island. I was not the only one. Their absence cast a shadow over the hope that should have come with continuing our journey. Despite our oaths and outward condemnations, there was a silent envy for their daring and a longing for the simple life that could have been ours under this foreign sun.

The attempt to celebrate Christmas amidst another wave of illness was a grim reminder of our plight. The Major did his best to institute some sense of sacredness. Bible verses were read, and spirits were provided as a Christmas treat. With the spirits came merriment, with the Major calling on the fiddlers, fifes, and drums to lead us in song and dance. After my share of rum, I did dance, which brought much delight. I hope never to be without the ability to dance, for it is then I feel the fullness of God and all of the life He has created within me. The Major even allowed those not essential on duty to play chess and cards well into the night. Despite the moments of mirth, with so many still sick, all of this enjoyment was embedded within the macabre ritual of death. The next day, with sore heads and sick stomachs, we still had to endure the duty of wrapping foul, decaying bodies and dumping them over the side.

There were moments when I questioned whether this journey was a punishment from the Lord for my past sins. There were things I had done with women before I left that, despite Uncle John's reassurance, I was sure that God would not condone. Or perhaps, this plight is a test of strength for the tasks He has planned for my future. I am mindful that I will only know this with certainty once I meet my maker. In my heart, I harbour the hope that my actions on this journey, with all its trials, its moments of frailty, will find favour in His eyes. I have endeavoured to navigate the moral tempests with the compass of His teachings, and I wish with all that I am it has been enough for Him to keep me as one of his flock.

And now, on the eve of our arrival, I stand here nervously awaiting my new chapter. I have heard the stories of harsh territories, deadly creatures, the chaos of the colony and of the unpredictable native peoples. Tomorrow, I step into the unknown only armed with the faith formed from making it thus far. I pray that the Lord's purpose for me in this land may become clear and that I may remember the grace He has shown in allowing me to step off this ship. May God grant me the strength to meet the days ahead with courage and wisdom, and may He stand by my side through whatever I may meet.

21 April 1792

Yesterday, I marked the beginning of my nineteenth year with what commenced as collegiate revelry and the sharing of a good dose of rum. However, as the liquor clouded the minds of my companions, the simple games we had before us would no longer satisfy them. In their drunken desires, my comrades strayed into excesses that I cannot condone. They ventured into the women's quarters, taunting me to join them. Those who have been here much longer than I advised that this is an accepted practice. But it is one in which I cannot partake and one that troubles me deeply. I am tasked with safeguarding these women from harmful predators, and I cannot use this privilege to justify personal indulgence. My role, as I see it, is to embody the honour of my lineage, not to betray the trust placed in me.

Seeing my friends, these officers, swagger towards the women's quarters, I was reminded of the harsh reality that breeds such behaviour. Each day, as I allocate food and clothing to settlers and convicts, I am confronted with the grim reality of scarcity that plagues our colony. Food, so essential for survival, is in perilously short supply. Hunger only breeds hate and desperate attempts to fill the holes. The women, in their vulnerability, emerge as the only source of manly pleasure in this isolated outpost, a role thrust upon them by circumstance rather than choice. Liquor is the only salve for the souls who have lost trust in the Holy Spirit. But it, too, leads to more violence and disrespect, particularly towards those we ought to protect.

Despite bearing the scars of their past, I deeply believe that these women deserve kindness. They are God's children, too, and no different from the mother and sisters I have left behind. Yet respect is a rare currency in these parts. Here, women are treated like produce. They are paraded like livestock, picked off by the bidder, and stripped of their dignity. They are not treated like chattels but something worth far less.

The quarters housing these women is a place of hardship that is difficult to articulate. Cramped and overcrowded, these spaces afford little in the way of privacy or comfort, with each woman allotted but a scant portion of space to call her own. The neglect paid to sanitation ensures that disease looms ever-present over the health and wellbeing of these women. Their rudimentary shelters offer scant protection against the wild weather, and I worry what may become of them in winter.

Under the watchful eyes of guards, their lives are regimented and controlled, every movement monitored, every freedom curtailed. They are forced to undertake labour that is both demanding and demeaning. Some, of good looks and temperament, are lucky to be taken into reputable homes. Still, it is well understood that they go there as concubines, trading favours for comfort. Their treatment, ranging from forced servitude to outright abuse, is a blight upon our conscience, a testament to the colony's capacity for cruelty.

Yet, amidst this bleakness, a spirit of friendship and fortitude prevails. I have seen these women sharing stories of suffering, laughter and tears and offering support, strength and solidarity. Through each other, they retain a solid sense of self when everything around them seeks to strip it away. Their resilience in the face of adversity commands my deepest respect.

I have heard whispers that some convict women have turned to ancient brews to assist them in personal acts of retaliation and revenge. Many stories are circulating about male abusers who have fallen gravely ill in the days and weeks that follow an act of abuse. It is suspected they were poisoned by those they have wronged. Such desperate measures, while indefensible, highlight a grim reality: when treated as less than human, people may embody the disdain cast upon them. This, to me, is a reflection not of their failure but of our collective moral downfall. The fear of illness or death has not reduced this practice, though. Anyone who has made the journey here is no longer afraid of death. In fact, it has strengthened their belief that they deserve some pleasure before their end, which, in this place, is likely near. I only pray that whatever witchcraft is employed may not be cast upon those involved in my birthday festivities. However, every choice has a consequence.

For while I consider what they did a sin, my sympathy extends to these men. I recognise the heavy burden the colony imposes upon our spirits. The colony's life is unforgiving, and in their quest for solace, some officers succumb to overindulgence. I cannot cast stones when my own conscience is in conflict. I will admit to admiring one convict girl of good age and character. Her beauty seems to cast away the gloom and offer some hope of happiness. I pray the Lord will keep me strong and not let me give in to this temptation, although with each day that passes, my resolve is reducing.

My sympathy for my comrades stops, though, when their excesses lead to violence. The fights, the brawls, the discord and division only serve to increase the hardships of our existence. In their pursuit of temporal pleasure, they merely perpetuate the cycle of despair. We are meant to be leaders of this colony, individuals entrusted with its safety and security. Yet, through our actions, we are exacerbating the colony's lawlessness. It pains me to say, but it appears that we are part of the problem.

Such concerns, though, are dulled during the day, which are filled with the duties of record-keeping, and managing the essentials that sustain our colony. There is no doubt that these tasks are burdensome, especially when what I have to give is not enough to satisfy. However, it also comes with the gift of humility. Being in front of these people allows me to touch the lives of settlers and convicts alike, and pass on the compassion of God with a semblance of humanity. In these acts, I find a purpose that transcends the baseness of our situation.

I am desperately missing my family, and await news from them each day. I am also missing the dear friends I had back at home in the horses. We always had a highland pony at home, and in its company, I always felt understood. The journey and conditions here in this new land have not been kind to the beautiful beasts that have come across the oceans. Breeding has been slow, and the colony only has one stallion, one mare and two colts. I hope and pray to have the opportunity to be moved into a position where I can care for these, the most majestic of God's creatures. How I would love to help them build a flourishing family, and I long desperately to care for another foal.

Major Grose's commendation of my court duties fills me with pride, for I strive to uphold fairness. Perhaps it is my father's legacy, one of unwavering integrity, that guides me. God rest his soul. He showed me what a sacred duty it is to administer justice and compassion. I consider it an honour indeed to do this here, in a land where such virtues are in short supply.

On this day, as I ponder the year ahead, I am burdened with a profound sense of responsibility—not merely to my superiors or those under my charge, but to the very essence of decency and respect that was instilled by my mother and is at the core of my being. It is a challenging path, fraught with perils, both moral and physical. Yet, it is one I choose to walk with resolve, hoping that through my deeds, I may contribute to a legacy of Christian compassion amidst the desolation of our existence.

TO THE HEART OF THE MAN

24 December 1792

As the eve of Christmas descends, I find myself incredibly weary. This heat is like being trapped in a sweltering sack. We experienced extreme temperatures along our voyage to this land, but then we had the ocean spray and breeze to cool our skins. Here, we have neither, and it has me longing for the Christmas I know back with my family. I now remember, with fondness, undertaking my chores in the frost, worrying that my fingers and toes were frozen and then flinging myself down in front of the hearth to warm my body. How good that fire felt. Here in New Holland, it is the fire that I am trying to escape, but there are few opportunities for respite. This sustained sense of being smothered is causing everyone to become cranky and sparking many conflicts. I wonder if I will acclimate to these foreign temperatures or whether I will always find this weather so uncomfortable. All I do know is that I have decided to keep my distance from those with light tempers.

This summer's dryness has also brought severe concerns for the ongoing sustainability of this settlement. The rivulet that meandered through our settlement and provided a source of fresh water has been reduced to a mere trickle. Its vitality, like mine, has been sapped by the unyielding sun. The soil, too, has proven a formidable adversary, with many crops around the colony failing to bring forth what was planned. The cackle of the Kookaburra, once a simple source of enjoyment, is now met with confusion. We are uncertain as to whether we should be excited, hoping their song may signal rain, or shun them for their cruel mockery of our circumstance.

We are fortunate that the fields in the Hawkesbury and Paramatta are fertile and flourishing, providing some sustenance. Still, the rations of vegetables, hardtack and salted meats are insufficient to keep everyone satisfied, and we are many more years away from full yield.

The presence of flies has become a constant source of irritation; their incessant buzzing and the way they swarm, undeterred, to blanket my back or dart into my face, is a test of my patience for which I constantly need to plead to the Lord to help me find. Sometimes, though, it also results in my asking for forgiveness when the cusses come out beyond my control. We are compelled to take meticulous care to protect our provisions from these pests, covering foodstuffs diligently to prevent them from being spoiled by maggots, a fate all too common in this climate.

There are additional threats to our provisions in the form of natives and bushrangers. Governor Phillip made incursions into the territory along Hawkesbury and excelled at understanding the natives and forming relationships with them. A weaker man would have wrought havoc when he was mistakenly speared by some scared natives, but his resistance against retaliation should be shown great respect. I greatly admire his approach of investigation and integrity rather than force and domination. I think this will put us in good stead as we seek to expand the settlement. I can only hope that our new administrator, Governor Grose, will also apply a philosophy of compassion towards the traditional people of this land.

Still, like our own people, it is impossible to control the hungry and desperate, and our transports offer easy pickings. Some convicts, like Black Caesar, have escaped and now seek to scavenge from others. I know many who find such a man an inspiration, an example of defiance against the injustice and inhumanity of the law and our leaders. Still, I consider them cowards. It is so much easier to steal the fruits of other people's labour than to grow them for yourself. I understand the sentiment that the spoils of this colony are unequally shared, and so their actions are a protest against the exclusives and their excesses. There are, however, heroic ways to fight injustice, and I do not classify the bushranger's actions as such.

I am willing to acknowledge that perhaps my perspective has been made more severe now that I am a landowner. I have now received twenty-five acres granted to me as a member of the Corp. My pride in this land, as little as it is, will see me protect it at all costs. For it is not just land to me but the beginning of a legacy for my family. I am adamant that I will transform my plot into a productive homestead. The soil, though, is challenging, and it will take a great deal of care to have it provide any substantial provisions for myself and much more work will be required for it to become an additional source of income from sales to the colony.

In the moments of toil, I find a newfound respect for the convicts I have been provided with to work this land. Like the labourers who visited the inn back home, they give so much of themselves to the act of creation. And like them, my body is so weary, and there is much temptation to have it buoyed by wine, women, and song.

There is not much wine here but plenty of rum, and I find the women increasingly harder to resist. I am no stranger to the ways of women, for while I was raised under my mother's staunch and righteous guidance, she also understood the realities of the age in which we lived. She never once judged the women who would visit our inns, seeking to exchange their bodies for the sources of survival. She would always treat them kindly and offer them care. We all knew that sex outside marriage was a sin and that it was meant for procreation and not pleasure. However, what was preached from the pulpit was very different to what was practical.

Our family was committed to following the commandments and did so within our own context. She did not criticise nor condone the women at the inn that showed me how to treat a lady. They did so not for their own benefit but to help me become a man. Uncle John, too, made sure that before I sailed, I had my fill. He did not want to see me away, to what may be my death, without knowing the ecstasies of the flesh and the fairer sex. Some days, I do yearn for the time before I knew the joys of women, for my ignorance would make this temptation so much easier to resist.

And I am struggling to restrain myself from being drawn into carnality with one convict girl. I see her as she comes to get rations, and her presence stirs within me a bluster of emotions. Though fraught with the potential for transgression, our encounters are moments of profound connection. Her beauty, paired with the wildness in her eyes, speaks of a spirit unbroken by her circumstances. In her, I see a reflection of this land's raw, untamed essence. Her name is Sarah, and she shares the same stoic yet shiny nature as my mother and sister, who also share her name. She has golden hair, which is simply enchanting. Sarah, too, has been here long enough to understand that the self-indulgence of the soldiers is standard and can also be a clever source of sponsorship. She knows that as a convict, it would be impossible to be taken as a wife. She will never be delivered as a decent woman. Yet she has made it strikingly clear that a dalliance with me is not only possible but inescapable. She tells me that our fates have been bound together, and to continue battling the calls of our flesh is futile. I pray that I hold steady to the moral compass that guides me and that the Lord may give me strength to not succumb to the demands of my desires.

I also beseech the Lord to shower blessings upon my mother and sisters and keep them safe from all harm. My heart aches with longing to hear from them and to see them once more. Without their humour, grace, and generosity, the days are arduous. Still, their memory strengthens my determination to make something of myself and to make them proud.

TO THE HEART OF THE MAN

12 May 1793

Under the competent command of Philip Gidley King, I have found my footing on the remote shores of Norfolk Island, a place as daunting as it is captivating. The generosity of Captain Macarthur and McKellar in swiftly securing my position here speaks volumes of their character, for which I am profoundly grateful. I am deeply indebted to them for their counsel, friendship and assistance to see me away at such short notice. King appears to be a strict but fair leader, seeming to have the welfare of all those on the island uppermost in his mind. I look forward to serving him the best that I can.

McKellar, a true friend and connection to the wider world, supplies me with essentials and news. His most recent shipment contained sugar, ribbons, and shoes and an update on the tumultuous events unfolding across the seas — the grim fate of Louis XVI and the precarious position of Marie Antoinette, alongside England's entanglement in war with France. While distant, the echoes of revolution, a people's clamour against decadence and corruption, also reflect the lives and struggles witnessed here. The Corps are also embarking on machinations to ensure their survival and prosperity. In Port Jackson there is increasingly becoming a great divide between those that have and those that have not. While some may see the Corps' undertakings as illegal, others argue their actions are essential to prevent the dangers of extreme inequality.

Here, Norfolk Island feels like a world away from the mainland. Though limited in size and beset by geographic hardships, this island is home to a community of some fifteen hundred souls. Its terrain, while inhospitable, yields generously under toil. The majestic Norfolk Pines dominate the landscape, their massive forms a constant reminder of God's magnificence.

It is a raw and beautiful place, perhaps too congenial for my penance. Still, there is no escaping the memory that my existence here is an act of self-abasement for my sinful actions with Sarah. I am followed with every step by the shadows of my weakness and will only return when I feel I have been forgiven. Although I will understand the Lord's decision if he would instead think it fit to escort me through the gates of hell. The weight of this shame is a constant companion, reminding me of my fragility in the face of temptation.

True, some of my comrades have conducted themselves far more indecently with their women than I did with Sarah. And Sarah was goading me to be less gentle and more of a man. There was no injury or cruelty, and Sarah and I remained constant afterwards, laughing and joining in the remaining birthday revelries. Coming down from the rum, my genuine enjoyment soon turned to guilt. While those around me celebrated my capitulation into the crudeness of the colony, I felt that instead, I had been condemned. Nay, neither my heart nor head can bear another birthday like the last.

The echoing calls of the ghost birds at night know the sorrow that I hold and help me mourn the death of my morality. The vivid flashes of the kingfisher by day and the friendly encounters with the Norfolk Robin offer fleeting distractions from the internal turmoil and a reminder that there is still much beauty on this earth.

Upon arrival, I heard that Black Caesar, once confined to this island, had returned to Port Jackson, leaving behind his wife and daughter in this harsh, isolated place. I ponder the desperation or resolve that could drive a man to abandon those most vulnerable. What drives a man to leave his family to fend alone in a land that offers little clemency?

I am only glad that McKellar has given up trying to convince me to return to the mainland and appears to have some empathy for my plight. It is best that I absent myself from further temptation. The girls in Port Jackson are too much for me. McKellar's retort is simple, stating that I must seek to become more of a man. But what they expect of me is not in my nature. Norfolk, it appears, is far more manageable for this fellow.

Being here, I am also excused from being directly engaged in Macarthur's schemes, which is of great relief. Macarthur is now moving to secure the power of the Corp over the colony's trade. He has found favour with Governor Grosse, a man also of the military and together they are controlling all consignments in and out of the ports. They are reaping a handsome profit from this endeavour, which they share generously with the Corp members. As part of the Corps, I, too, will benefit from this political activity, although with it, I have many personal concerns. I fear it is leading to further division and disparity in the colony. Yet, it is also the pathway to a secure future for me and the family I yearn to build. If it were not us making money from these material transactions, then the traders would be the ones profiting. Therefore, I do believe it is better within our pockets than theirs. I admire Macarthur for his vision, audacity and unwavering commitment to our collective prosperity. I must concede, against my gnawing conscience, that my aspirations have become intertwined with Macarthur's rise.

20 August 1793

The news delivered through McKellar's latest correspondence has struck me with a force that has unsettled my very foundations. I am to be a father. The revelation that Sarah is with child has plunged me into a wild sea of emotions. I am blessed, though, to have two steadfast companions in this storm, The Lord and Lieutenant King, and I seek their counsel constantly.

My days, filled with the challenges of assisting Lieutenant Philip Gidley King in establishing a sustainable community, have imbued my life with a sense of purpose and passion. The struggle to coax sustenance from the unforgiving soil and to build a semblance of civilisation in this wild place is arduous and unrelenting. And yet, it is the highest of honour to be of service and to use my time to improve the lot of these people. I do so surrounded by the majesty of God's creation, the vast sea and sky, the colourful creatures and towering pines all work to ease my torment.

Despite the splendour of this place and the fullness of my days, I still find my mind and heart filled with Sarah, the risks of this situation and the responsibilities that I must uphold. I know that childbirth, daunting in the best of times, is, in these remote conditions, fraught with peril. The colony has already lost women and children in this way. The medical facilities are rudimentary at best, resources are scarce, and the threat of disease is ever-present. The reality of mortality looms large over every pregnant woman and her unborn child. Macarthur's wife, Elizabeth, a truly beautiful soul, has told me about the loss of her child on the journey to Port Jackson. I can tell that it still hurts and haunts her. My heart aches at the thought of losing Sarah, the baby, or both, with me being the ultimate cause of their fate and being too far away to offer any assistance. The decision to flee is feeling now less noble and increasingly cowardly. Am I truly no better than Black Caesar?

I am also plagued with anxiety over how I may provide for Sarah and our child. My wage is still only modest, and how can I ensure their wellbeing from afar? When the time comes, I may need to call on the assistance of my dear friends McKellar and Macarthur to arrange for some of my salary to be siphoned to her. For there is, in this colony, no clear way to make Sarah an honourable woman. Marrying a convict, while not illegal, is socially unacceptable and would condemn my career. It depresses me to think that siring an illegitimate child is seen as less sinful than publicly declaring her as your dependant. It harks to the hell in which these convict women find themselves; to provide for the desires of the men, but to know that they themselves may never be provided for.

In dealing with this dilemma, my thoughts meander to my own father, lost to me when I was eleven. I recall the anguish of my mother as we buried him and the reverence with which the townsfolk spoke of him. He was a vintner, farmer, and respected bailie in our small Scottish town. From what I can remember, he was heralded as a man of virtue. Sometimes, he would have Thomas and I attend his hearings to watch him as he presided over the local court. In the evening, he would discuss the reasons behind his adjudication, showing how his resolution was based on fairness and respect for all parties. His allocation of taxes to public projects was always astute, and he upheld the standards of trade to ensure a balanced benefit for all. I also witnessed his efforts to care for the poor, his concern during outbreaks of disease, and his endeavours to ensure access to clean water and essential services. In times of public celebration and in moments of private despair, he stood as a leader, guiding our community with a steady hand.

Reflecting on the life my father led, the respect he garnered, and the legacy he left behind, I am struck by the parallels in the path I now tread. Here on Norfolk Island, under the command of Lieutenant Philip Gidley King, I find myself drawn to the challenges of establishing a sustainable community and striving for justice. Still, this land is so far removed from the world which my father served. At night, I lay in bed and wonder what he would have done if he, too, found himself in this foundling community. I do not dare to consider though what he would make of my current predicament, casting a convict girl into peril and then absenting myself from the whole affair.

Sometimes, I seek silent counsel from Uncle John, asking myself what he would do in my situation. Uncle John has taken the reigns of fatherhood and has been my role model for the last eight years. He has provided me with this ensign, clothed me in a way befitting to this position, and showed me the ways of an officer and a gentleman. He organised for me to be held back in London so that I may attend the Academy, a privilege that mere words cannot describe how greatly I appreciate. I have cause to smile as I remember Uncle John telling the Academian that I was the best dancer in London, and the Academian retorting that he wished I applied the same attention to arithmetic. My greatest wish is to create a life here in the new world where there is much time for dancing. It is a vice that I learnt at the hands of the audacious Master William Gregg, perfected at the Red Lion and do truly miss. Dancing now, though, while Sarah struggles, seems an act far too decadent and indecent.

In the quiet of the evening, I reflect upon the courage and integrity of my father and Uncle John and pledge to uphold their example. I have made a grave mistake and will take responsibility, just as they would, and make whatever amends I can. For Sarah, our child and the father who taught me duty and compassion, I will strive to build a future where all can flourish. I pray that the Lord keeps Sarah and our baby safe and that my father's soul is resting in peace.

25 December 1793

On this Christmas Day, under the vast skies of Norfolk Island, I find myself reflecting on the year's hardships and blessings. On the eve of the Lord's birth, there was a small mass for the colony's inhabitants, and today, the celebrations are simple. Christmas here is marked not by any opulence but by a shared sense of community. Some people have made gifts from whatever they could gather, and these are given with sincere thankfulness for the little we have. Our meal was no different from other days, with no added luxuries available. We dined on salted pork and mutton birds, which are becoming an ever-increasing staple. The vegetables are still sparse, a constant reminder of the challenges of cultivating this land. As we shared stories of Christmas past and the contrasts that this day brings, I could sense that while, on the surface, the storytelling had buoyed our spirits, far within each one of us, it had also stirred a deep sense of sorrow.

The recent correspondence from McKellar brought news that warmed my heart and gave me much reason for hope. Through the efforts of Macarthur and him, I have been granted an additional one hundred and ten acres in Parramatta. This land, with its promise of rich soil and potential for bountiful harvests, fills me with anticipation. The thought of cultivating it, of turning it into prosperous farmland, fuels my determination to fulfil my duties here and promptly return to the mainland to make something great of the opportunity I have been afforded. Having not one but two pieces of land to my name now opens doors to greater income, an elevated status within the colony, and, most importantly, the means to provide for Sarah and my future family. McKellar has also advised that from what he can gather, Sarah's pregnancy is progressing well. The child is expected in the new year. I will not be there to see it enter this harsh world, and I do not know when I will return to fulfil my responsibility to care for it as a new member of the colony. I have resolved to find a way to do what is right and be a father, whatever form that may take.

There are murmurings, though, that all of us may be forced from Norfolk Island soon. This place has many blessings but has no safe harbour and has failed to be self-sustaining. With resources being stretched on the mainland, there is a decreasing desire to continue supporting this post, so it may be shut down. It is an experiment they are no longer willing to fund. There were such high hopes for the flax crops we had planted, and which would have been a bountiful source of revenue. We would have established a sail-making industry on the island, securing exports and boosting our economy. But these plantings have failed to be anything more than a disappointment. It has been a similar result for the timbers that were to be the beginning of a mast-building industry. They, too, have been proven to be incapable of delivering on the dreams we held. The realisation that these assets will reap no rewards casts a serious shadow over our future.

This setback, I fear, only adds to our sense of isolation and the growing discontent among the population. Daily, I witness the strain of survival here. King describes the situation so aptly when he remarks that there is discord and strife etched into every face. The scarcity of food breeds a desperation that I fear may lead to turmoil, for hunger and hate are fast friends. Our reliance on mutton birds is a stark reminder of our precarious existence. Without these creatures, the tenuous bonds of our civilisation would surely break. They are surely stretched, and I wonder how much longer they can hold. In these moments of doubt and concern for the future, my faith becomes my fortress. I find my strength in the Lord.

As I pen this entry, my thoughts turn to Sarah and our unborn child. I find myself whispering a prayer into the warm night air, a plea for their safety and wellbeing. May the Lord watch over them during the birth, granting them strength and shielding them from harm.

TO THE HEART OF THE MAN

20 April 1794

Easter on Norfolk Island, in the year of our Lord 1794, has been an occasion of profound reflection. The day was marked by a simple yet solemn service, where we gathered, united in faith. This small community has turned to the resurrection of Jesus as a symbol of hope that our fates, too, may rise and come to a new and full life on this island. This sentiment is deeply needed in these challenging times as we deal daily with the stresses of survival and sustaining the many lives under our care, convicts and settlers alike.

Adding to the air of celebration, this Easter coincides with the commemoration of my twenty-first birthday—a coincidence that I am unsure will ever happen again in my lifetime. Captain King's thoughtful gesture made the day all the more memorable. In the act of kindness that speaks to his considerate character, he ordered a birthday cake to be made in my honour. Amid our austerities, such a treat is a rare luxury, and its meaning has not been lost on me, for we seem to be forming a friendship beneath the rigours of our formal responsibilities.

Captain King, a Cornishman like myself, has proven to be a sound administrator, giving his all to care for his people. His good humour in times of tension has been a great source of relief, even if much of it comes at my expense. He heartily jokes about my poor prospects of marriage. Instead, he suggests that given the level of attention directed at me by the island's women, I would be more suited to a harem.

There is much to admire about this man, though, including his determination and decisiveness. He is also making great advancements for the betterment of all on the island. Recently, he has established a court. While others have suggested this is merely for the escalation of his own power, it has added greatly to the air of law and order in this community. It has also endowed me again with the privilege of court duty, an opportunity to demonstrate sound judgment and contribute further to the governance of our island society. This responsibility fills me with pride and a sense of purpose as I strive to uphold the values of fairness and justice.

King has also arranged for horses and livestock to be delivered to the island, bringing great hope that through the aid of these animals, we may provide sufficient food for our people. There is much joy with the thought that we will have something other than mutton bird to eat. I am also delighted with the idea that I may again be around the Arabians and Andalusians I admired in London. At night, I imagine racing across the island's plains, feeling the power of the hooves pounding the earth and the rush of freedom in my chest. My heart aches to be around horses again. I hope to one day possess a thoroughbred of my own, a creature of grace, strength and integrity, and the truest of friends.

Under King's stewardship, the colony has seen the construction of much essential infrastructure. He will not let the looming thought of this colony's closure prevent his people from receiving the services that he believes to be their God-given rights. Over the past few months, King has set about establishing a new gaol, a school, a hospital, a surgeon's house, a bakehouse, a grain shed, and a storeroom. These structures stand as a symbol of the vision King has of prosperity and community for all who call Norfolk Island home. He has not given up and still rallies us to make the dreams a reality.

It is a pity, though, that King's character is marred by his malicious temper. Many of us worry it is but a symptom of the tortuous gout that he is battling. The sight of his face turning red in anger may be seen as a sign of the blazing fire in his joints. His voice thundering with authority may be a result of his loss of patience with the politics, but also of the pain pulsing within his own body. King's angry outbursts have not yet resulted in any physical injury, and I believe they are a small, if not terrifying, price to pay for the security and progress he has brought to our community. He barks loudly but has very little bite.

His stress may also have been the impetus for his introduction of a weekly play, which we all must gather to watch. Dr Balmain has been put in charge of the theatre and his presentations have become a greatly longed-for source of light-heartedness. Of course, these performances are nothing like the vibrant ones I experienced in Covent Garden, and the atmosphere of the Norfolk Island Playhouse can never begin to reflect the opulence and liveliness that its London counterpart encompasses. Still, it is one step towards instilling some culture in this colony and a skilful means to distract us from the distress of our dire surroundings and uncertain future.

24 May 1795

The grip of winter is beginning to tighten around Norfolk Island, its cold breath seeping into my bones. As the weather changes, I too find myself on the verge of a significant shift. I have been called to return to the mainland. Governor Grose has departed the colony, and his deputy Patterson, awaiting the arrival of the new Governor Hunter, is eager to strengthen the Corp's presence and put on a good show. This news has stirred such extremes of emotions. I have such pride for all I have accomplished in this rugged outpost and for the friendships forged, of which I will count Captain King amongst them. Leaving these endows me with a sense of melancholy, especially given the tenuous nature of King's health.

The gout has tightened its grip over King, rendering him a prisoner within his own body. The disease, merciless in its assault, compresses his lungs, making every breath an effort and subjects him to constant, gnawing pain in his stomach. Our conversations, once filled with plans for the future, now often turn to darker musings on the fragility of life and what may come of his legacy on this island. The leeches and poultices seem to be doing very little to provide ease, and I fear that the reliance he has formed on spirits to dull his pains may only be adding to his woes.

The stress of the conflict that occurred with Governor Grose severely deepened his affliction. While Grose has now gone, the damage has been done. I see in King's troubles the heavy burden that leadership imposes and the personal toll it extracts. I am also becoming increasingly aware of how much our circumstance rests on the countenance of the Governor of the time. The Governor can make or break a man, and I fear Grose succeeded in doing the latter. The reproof Grose gave King when he left Norfolk to return the Māori to New Zealand was scathing, suggesting that he had abandoned his duties. King would never do such a thing. The journey was used to advance our interests, however Grose savagely smothered this in a load of false failings.

The behaviour of the NSW Corp has also caused more conflict. When a gang of drunken troublemakers from the Corp set upon Mrs King's servants and then had the audacity to spit on King himself, we all knew these soldiers had gone too far. I could not support my comrades in this act of indecency. Luckily, I was not alone in my condemnation. The rest of the Corps on the island supported King's decision to send the twenty mutineers back to the mainland for trial by court-martial. It was a sentence the remainder of us considered just. Grose, though, attacked King for being unduly harsh to the soldiers and favouring the convicts. In retaliation, he granted the military authority over the island. King had been sidelined, and I am sure the stress of witnessing the cruel hand of military rule would have fuelled the great fire within.

What troubled me most in watching the war between King and Grose was seeing how great men sat on either side of the conflict. Each, in their own way, had noble intentions. I know that Grose worked hard to support Macarthur and ensure the prosperity of the Corps, for which I am thankful. However, I also understand the need to construct a civilian community that can sustain itself, and I support King in this endeavour. Knowing who I must side allegiance with is a constant source of anxiety and one that I will need to navigate on my return.

I do not know the new Governor, Hunter, personally. Yet, the reputation of this old Scot precedes him. Hunter has had years of distinguished service in the Navy and, by all accounts, fought bravely in the American War of Independence and successfully applied his strategic acumen in the skirmishes against the French. He has great battle experience and will be a formidable adversary to Macarthur and the Corps. There is no doubt a great deal of apprehension as to how this new relationship will play out and who will secure power.

Macarthur has woven his influence and the Corp deep into the fabric of the colony. We now control much of the trade and have the convict labour to use to our advantage. This creates a significant economic advantage for the Corp and their dependents and threatens the once guaranteed comfort of the exclusives. It is understandable that the powers within the motherland would like to restore the balance to the elite, and unsurprising that they are sending Hunter to spur change.

However, through Macarthur's cunning and Grose's compliance, the Corp is now in charge of the courts. It is this action of Macarthur's that challenges my conscience greatly. I worry that it has turned justice into a commodity, traded as deftly as the goods that pass through Port Jackson. On my return, I hope to play a role in the courts again, doing all I can to ensure justice and compassion are not compromised for commercial gains. I have no doubt, though, that the courts will become a brutal battleground between these two men as they both seek supremacy over life and law.

There is so much apprehension brewing about the return to Port Jackson. Yet there is also anticipation. I am eager to reunite with the land I own and embark upon my own agricultural venture. The prospect of tending to my estate, sinking my hands into the earth and coaxing life from the soil fills me with a sense of purpose. My mind races with plans for planting wheat, and I even imagine standing on my property in the future, watching the golden stalks sway in the breeze. I may also have space for maize or the chance to begin an orchard, growing citrus and apples. I suspect the climate may not be conducive to grapes, but I still dream of a land covered in vines, heavy and ready for harvesting. There may be a chance to establish a wine industry and follow in my father's footsteps as a vintner. There is so much opportunity ahead, and it fills me with great excitement. I pray that I live long enough to leverage the fruits of this land and build a great legacy.

It is with both sadness and relief that I received the news of Sarah's move to the Hawkesbury settlement, taking with her our daughter, named for her mother, Sarah Ann. It appears I am to spend my days surrounded by Sarahs. It is the name of my mother, sister, the mother of my child, and now my daughter. It is not lost on me that God called Abraham to leave his country and become the founder of a new nation and that he did so with Sarah at his side. Sarah was given the privilege to be the mother of nations, and in their own way, the Sarahs that I have in New Holland are also fulfilling this sacred duty. I only pray that God may see fit to bless my descendants as he did those of Abraham and Sarah.

As I bid farewell to Norfolk Island, with its haunting beauty and deep connections forged in the face of shared trials, I carry the lessons learned from King. The journey back to the mainland is undertaken with mixed feelings, but recognised as an opportunity to fulfil many long-held dreams. I pray that the Lord will keep all of my darling Sarahs safe. May He also see fit to show this colony some compassion and cure King's condition.

TO THE HEART OF THE MAN

4 September 1797

As the seasons turn I have finally received the news that my request for leave has been granted. And so, the spring also heralds my departure back to Scotland. The thought of seeing my mother, sisters, and brother again warms my heart and fills me with such hope, for it has been a gruelling span of two years since I arrived back from Norfolk Island. They have been years marked by the tempestuous tenure of Governor Hunter and the relentless and sinister scheming of my friend, John Macarthur.

The conflict between Hunter and Macarthur has marred this colony, drenching it in struggles over power and profit, within which I, by association with the Corps and Macarthur, have found myself entangled. The institutions and systems of control that Macarthur and Grose constructed have been extremely successful and significantly improved my financial situation. Still, they also cast a shade upon my soul, for they are founded upon a clear departure from the moral principles I once held dear and swore to myself that I would always uphold. This colony seems to have a way of twisting you until you fit in with whatever power rules the day. And it is obvious to all that in this struggle Macarthur is the stronger.

The most disheartening spectacle has been the degradation of our legal system. I have seen it defaced and now designed as a tool for personal vendettas. The incident involving our chief surgeon, Doctor Balmain, and his call for justice in the assault of a civilian by Macarthur's men stands as a stark stand to the corruption that festers within. Macarthur's public humiliation of the doctor, coupled with the ominous threats from some of his officers, is nothing short of a decay in moral integrity. Macarthur will not accept this assessment, simply stating there are things that must be done to maintain order.

Hunter, though, is no innocent party in this distressing duel. He dismissed Macarthur as Inspector of Public Works, an act I am sure he would have known would lead to severe retaliation. However, he seemed completely unprepared for the resulting cruel campaign that Macarthur instituted to discredit Hunter with the British government. I don't think anyone foresaw that Macarthur would stoop so low to attribute the widespread drunkenness in the colony to the Governor when it is clearly caused by the Rum Corp's own self-serving practices.

It was wise for Macarthur to leave the Corps when he did, to jump, one might say, before he was pushed. He sees much more profit achievable through agriculture. I wish him sincerely well in this endeavour and hope he may also assist me in further expanding my holdings. Despite his many shortcomings, Macarthur has a level of nous that no one else possesses, especially myself. And I will need this intelligence to rise to the station that I seek for my future family. I do wonder what will come of both men, Macarthur and Hunter, during my absence, which is intended to be two years. If there is one thing I do know, this colony will be much changed when I return.

Amidst all the turmoil over the past two years, I have found a sense of peace and purpose in the cultivation of my land. The convicts under my charge are generous labourers, and I have developed a deep regard for their resilience. The food production from my fields not only benefits the colony but adds to my fortunes, which I willingly share with those under my charge. This increased prosperity is also establishing the foundation for a family, a future now within grasp.

With my more solid financial footing, I have also set about providing for my daughter. Macarthur occasionally has cause to visit the fledging settlement in the Hunter and checks in on them on my behalf. On last report, they are both in somewhat favourable conditions, at least better than the convict women's quarters in this colony. Sarah has found a position as a housekeeper, although, on Macarthur's suggestion may be suffering from melancholy. His casual observation of my daughter's beauty and attribution of it to her father's lineage brings a rare smile in these trying times.

Though years from completion, the construction of the Church also gives me cause to rejoice and a heart full of hope. It will allow us a place to come together to worship and grow as a community under the cross of our Lord. I look forward to accompanying my family to the Church of my forefathers when I return to my homeland and sitting with a community that lives and breathes Christian principles. I pray that spending time around their prudence may bolster my own and that they may help me find a way to enable morality and ambition to coexist.

At the age of twenty-four, I stand at a crossroads. I do desire a family of my own, and yet I feel there is much more to accomplish before I can ensure a deserving future for my dependents. Macarthur's financial acumen has been essential to counter my inexperience. While the man has many faults, his guidance and stewardship of my affairs indicate there are limits to his evil and confirm the depth of our friendship. His wife, Elizabeth, is also, apart from my own mother, the most wonderful woman I have ever had the good fortune to meet. She is a stalwart, endowed with both intellect and virtue, and I am truly honoured to count her as a friend and confidant.

I have the greatest admiration for Elizabeth as she maintains her principles within the chaos of this colony, a feat that I have so far been unable to accomplish. Her companionship has been a source of comfort and enlightenment, offering a glimpse into the strength and potential of the women who stand alongside the men shaping this colony. I see her trying to balance her husband's improprieties, but by my assessment, her angelic attributes far outweigh Macarthur's misfeasance.

As I prepare again to endure the treacherous voyage, thoughts of the women in my family also arise, as do the fears for how I may find them. Mary's devotion is unparalleled. She is now twenty-seven and as unyet unmarried, dedicating herself solely to Mother and the Inn. Hannah is not married either, although she is still within an appropriate age range, and I am advised there are a number of prospects. Perhaps I can find her a suitable husband during my stay. It would be a wonderful gift to be able to leave her with a source of support. Margaret is now twenty-five and wed to Patrick Sloan, a local farmer. I am cautious about Sloan, hearing murmurings of cruelty towards his horses. I hope to assuage my anxiety about this soon. My little sister Sarah is also now married to John Allison. It is hard to imagine her as a wife, as she will always be my little Sarah. Fanny has done the best for herself, making a very advantageous match and marrying a surgeon. There is no doubt then that I will have to wear all of my decorations when I meet his clan.

TO THE HEART OF THE MAN

21 December 1798

Today, I make the final preparations for our departure from Hillsborough, accompanied on the return journey to New Holland by my brother, Hugh. My soul is enveloped by melancholy at having to leave my mother and sisters once more, and yet I am steadfast in my responsibility to be a role model for my brother. Hugh, following in the footsteps I have laid down in the Marines, will be my companion in this uncertain journey. Securing his commission, I have ensured that we shall stand shoulder to shoulder as we face what I already know to be a vast and unforgiving sea.

My recent sojourn in the countryside of my homeland and amongst the companionship of my family has been a balm to my weary spirit. As I watched the ever-changing tapestry of the seasons, I had time to contemplate the nature of life itself. I watched each transition from the vibrant bloom of spring to the golden tranquillity of summer, followed by the fiery leaves of autumn and the solemn purity and silence of winter. Here, I had space to reflect on my time so far in New Holland and what I hope to achieve on my return.

The natural splendour of the surroundings brought more sharply into contrast the accelerated aging of my beloved mother. It was soon after my arrival that I realised the profound possibility that this may be the last time I get to embrace her, dance with her, make her laugh and seek her wisdom. The years have woven a network of worry upon her face, marking the passage of seasons she has weathered in my absence. Mary, solid in her strength, has seamlessly assumed the role of our family's caretaker. I know she hides her yearning for children and her sorrow for this forbidden future. She shields us all from her sadness by lavishing us with love.

The time I spent in the company of my sisters and their spouses was a blessing that I will treasure forever. However, I do leave with many worries. Fanny's advantageous marriage to the surgeon is marred by an undercurrent of severity in his demeanour. He is not rough or rude, and yet there is an attitude that kindles concern within me. I have counselled Fanny to tread with caution and urged the sisters to remain vigilant in their mutual support and protection.

Our walks through the countryside, sometimes in convivial groups, other times in quiet pairings, have allowed for the exchange of many fears and hopes. It was during one such ramble that Hugh confided his apprehensions about military life. His vulnerability reminded me of my own unvoiced fears when I first beheld the Pitt and the heartache I withheld on the journey to New Holland. This shared moment of brotherly solidarity felt so significant, providing me with the chance to be both confidant and counsellor. I now have the chance to offer Hugh the support I once found so elusive and to be the big brother that I had always hoped I could be.

The nights spent in the Inn, alive with bawdy revelry, singing, and dancing, have rekindled the fire of family within. I cherished being surrounded by the community who would join us each evening, enveloping me in their warm embrace. Amongst these people, I could just be John and enjoy the simple pleasures. It made me contemplate whether I truly wanted to return to the colony Before my departure, I repainted the Red Lion sign, hanging above the door, and prayed that it may offer all inside protection and peace.

I leave with the subject of my daughter, Sarah Ann, remaining a secret. I did not dare share with my mother how I had taken a convict girl out of wedlock and sired a bastard child. The weight of my responsibility towards the Sarahs back in New Holland is a burden I carry alone. I will spare my mother any additional heartache that my choices might inflict.

I pray, Lord, watch over my cherished family in Maybole, shield them from harm, and envelop them in your boundless grace. As Hugh and I embark on a journey that may be our last, I ask that you keep us under Your watchful eye. We are trusting in Your mercy, My Lord. May Your light illuminate our path and Your strength sustain us through the months of hell ahead. And if my mother does pass from this Earth before I can return, please take her to be with you in Heaven.

TO THE HEART OF THE MAN

25 July 1799

The silhouette of the Hillsborough looms in the distance, and I, like all its other passengers, cannot escape from its sinister shadow fast enough. All who travelled aboard this ship and made it to this shore are still in shock. It was harrowing. It was horrific.

The ominous signs began as soon as we departed from Portland. Tempestuous weather battered the decks, overwhelming them with the sea, drenching the convicts' quarters and extinguishing any remnants of warmth. The snarling, relentless waves were but a prelude to the nightmare yet to unfold as typhoid; a silent stowaway began its grim reaping.

Death was a constant on my first journey on the Pitt, and there were some souls lost on my way back to Maybole. But what occurred on the Hillsborough was akin to slaughter, and I consider Master Hingston, nothing better than a murderer. It was revealed to me a few days after our departure that Hingston knew of the typhoid outbreak at the prison. Still, he chose to take convicts from this place, and in doing so, he contaminated the ship and condemned almost one hundred souls to the sea.

The voyage spanned a gruelling two hundred and twelve days and has etched deep scars upon my soul and that of my brother, Hugh. We now try to reconcile what we have witnessed and wonder what role we may play, if any, in the retribution against the recklessness of Hingston and his crew. At the same time, I must ensure I send my great regards to the Surgeon, Doctor Kunst. He tried to warn Hingston about the impending crisis, and to make him see sense.

But his concerns were cast aside by Hingston, who was sure we would manage whatever would unfold before us. His idea of management, though, was nothing short of malicious. The conditions on board were a horrendous display of the extent of human cruelty. The convicts, shackled and deprived of their humanity, were reduced to living in squalor, their rations and dignity stripped away by a master more concerned with profit than the sanctity of life. Our early days were marred by punishment and fear, a regime of starvation and isolation under the guise of discipline. There were whispers of mutiny by men who had been pushed further than any mortal should be by another human. However, word got back to Hingston, and his response was swift and brutal – lashes were meted out, blood stained the decks, and the instigators were put in neck braces. Their rations were so severely reduced that we all surmised Hingston was scheming to starve them to death for their treachery.

Before we even arrived at Table Bay, a grim toll of thirty souls had been committed to the deep. The doctor did all he could. I watched as he stayed up all night for the chance to sneak water to those who were ill, risking Hingston's wrath and lashes if he were caught. The doctor could not save them, though. The bodies of the dead were thrust into the sea, their passing unmarked by prayers or rites. Such a lack of respect was a convenience for a captain devoid of mercy and yet an act I find unforgivable. Seeing these sea burials, Hugh was shaken to his core. There is no more innocence left in my brother. He disembarked strongly, for that is what is expected of a Piper, but there is no doubt he is broken.

The decision to anchor in Table Bay brought no respite, only the continuation of a macabre dance with death. There were at least another hundred convicts ill, with many dying each day. While provisions were sourced, details of the disease on board were sent to the port administrators. Our presence became a blight upon the bay, and we were ordered to move to another location. Hingston tried to hide the extent of the horror by burying a number of the recently dead in the harbour. His deception did not work, and in a few days, as we maintained our mooring, we all watched as the rotting corpses washed back onto the shore. Kunst was able to arrange for the ill to receive treatment. There was no hospital though, simply an old stable with no fireplace, windows or lavatory. We left almost a month later after burying fifty of our own at the Cape.

Governor Hunter was appalled when he saw the survivors of this sadistic voyage walk by. I heard he described them as the most wretched he had ever seen. I only wish he could get some sense of what these people felt like. For his words do little justice to the depth of their suffering. I have heard Hingston was reported for dumping more bodies overboard before we berthed in an attempt to cover up his incompetence and cruelty. Now, I truly hope justice will be served for all those who suffered so much at this man's savage hands.

On board the ship, Hugh and I feared daily for our lives. We stayed close together, constantly checking for fever, afraid that any tiny fluctuation in temperature signalled the worst. I could have coped with falling ill and handed over my fate to God. But I could not have survived losing Hugh. We were spared, though, and I can only think it is due to God having another purpose in mind for us.

Hugh and I now sit, sheltering in each other's company as we try to make some sense of what we have witnessed. We both started this journey with faith in mankind and the belief that within each one was the heart of Jesus. Now, we are compelled to consider the reality that there may be men who have been taken by the devil himself. If so, Hingston is surely one.

I feel such pain for my brother. Hugh walked off the ship half the size of the man that stepped aboard but with an understanding, a worldliness that now looms well beyond his years. He has been diminished in health and stature through this journey, but more than this, his belief in God has been brought into question. His eyes are now open to the complexities and cruelty of this world. I understand how this ordeal does dampen one's faith, but I hope it will not be destroyed, and in time that it will be restored. It feels somewhat selfish, but in comforting Hugh, in consoling him through this hardship, I have found my purpose reaffirmed, and my heart healed. It has now become clear to me what I must do. Just as I have done for my dear brother, I must now care for my daughter. The Lord has spared me from the floating tomb and shown me that I am ready to fulfil my responsibilities as a father.

TO THE HEART OF THE MAN

21 October 1799

By the grace of providence, my circumstances have flourished beyond measure. In His infinite mercy, the Lord has seen fit to elevate my financial standing threefold. I have secured an increase in salary, the yields from my land have become bountiful, and the Corp's ventures have become vastly profitable. These blessings have now provided me with the means to introduce a semblance of domestic stability into my life, a foundation upon which I can build a future for my beautiful daughter.

I have now secured a small officer's house and employed the services of a housekeeper, Sarah Hughes, to add to the suite of beautiful Sarahs already within my heart. She is a woman of steadfast character and industrious nature and, as yet, has no children of her own. Her attire is modest, only what I can afford to provide for one in such a role. Yet Elizabeth has assured me that while it is simple, it is also respectable. She keeps her hair neatly bound, embodying the virtues of diligence and care that have become an indispensable support as I climb the ladder of society.

Hugh makes misguided jests on his frequent visits, referring to her as my concubine. This is a term unbefitting her station and contribution to our household, and I have made it clear that such language holds no place within the sanctity of our home. Hugh retorts with the reality that this is what they are - recorded as such in the population ledgers. I hope I have sufficiently made him understand that Sarah is not only here as a carer for my child but also as a companion for me, and therefore, both her and her position must be treated with respect.

Our house, a structure of wood and stone, though modest by England gentry standards, is arranged with a practical elegance. Wooden floors, sparsely covered with rugs, and walls adorned with trinkets provide a backdrop to the realities of our life, which is still rugged but becoming increasingly refined. Sarah Hughes navigates this space efficiently, her role extending beyond mere cleaning and cooking to encompass the nurturing of Sarah Ann. The presence of my daughter has made this house my home and has transformed my heart. Sometimes, I look at her and feel ashamed for not sharing her existence with my mother. For I know that my mother would love her just as much as I do.

Sarah Ann is now a tender five years of age and looks like an earthly angel in her simple blue cotton smock. Her small bonnet, a somewhat substandard shield against the sun's glare, is like a halo for her precious face. Her baptism in St. Phillip's Church was the proudest moment in my life thus far. With this sacred rite, Sarah Ann was both formally recognised as my daughter and welcomed into God's family. As I watched her being anointed, she was illuminated by the soft light filtering through small windows, a setting so beautiful and so fitting for such a significant ceremony. I have dear Elizabeth to thank for the white gown my daughter wore, a symbol of the protection and guidance she is afforded by the Almighty and many prominent people.

My heart swelled as I watched her being brought into the fold of God's family, taking my name and the assurance of a future secured by faith. I pray that, under the watchful eyes of Sarah Hughes and Elizabeth Macarthur and within the nurturing embrace of our household, Sarah Ann will grow to embody the virtues of grace, compassion, and strength.

I hope the stability and care provided by our house will shield our housekeeper, Sarah Hughes, from the harsher realities of life in the colony. It is well known that convict women are often compelled to become involved in the lucrative yet dangerous trade in spirits. This is a necessity for some but threatens their very lives and is ruinous to their good nature. I pray that the remuneration I provide will suffice, allowing her to live with dignity and without recourse to the unsavoury aspects of the colonial economy.

I beseech the Almighty to keep my family in Maybole safe and to watch over Sarah Hughes, Sarah Ann and Hugh as we navigate the challenges and joys of this colony. May He grant us the strength to uphold His teachings and to extend His love and mercy to all who cross our threshold.

TO THE HEART OF THE MAN

2 January 1801

As summer unfolds its bright sky over Port Jackson, the air, heavy with the scent of eucalypts and the sun's warmth, heralds another season of transformation. Blustery changes are blowing through the heart of our colony, stirred by King's return as Governor. While I had been hoping for a period of relative peace, I am heartened to see that King has regained his health, for when I left him last, I considered him close to death.

For my service and support on Norfolk Island, King has promoted me to Captain, and I am greatly honoured. However, I am deeply conflicted, for I know that this title comes with many expectations, including to assist him in overthrowing the control of Macarthur and the Corps. And so now I am ensnared in a web of conflicting loyalties.

The Governor shared with me his disgust at the prevailing conditions and his vision for the colony. Although, he is doing much more than merely talking. King is acting like a man possessed, immediately implementing sweeping reforms. King is determined to overhaul the system of administration and is not deterred by the looming spectre of discontent. Nevertheless, it is clear that the changes he seeks to make, while being beneficial for the long-term future of the colony, are to compromise my own financial security.

With the zeal of a man on a divine mission, King has unfurled a series of decrees aimed at dismantling the corruption he believes is at the centre of the Corp. He is taking bold steps to regulate the port and curb the import of spirits, keen to reinstate an air of temperance and greater economic equity. He also plans to establish a brewery and a public warehouse, seeking to quench the colonists' thirst for both wholesome libation and fair commerce. An edict will allow a markup of only fifty per cent above the cost of goods, well below the five hundred per cent markup the Corp places on several necessary items. King is also setting about pardoning a great many convicts, creating a vast new settler community. I know all of this will be a positive step forward for the people. Still, it severely undermines the profits upon which I have come to rely.

King's vision, however, extends well beyond the mere regulation of trade. He has shown me his holistic approach to colony building and his blueprint for a sustainable future. As much as I know I will suffer if they are successful, I am truly impressed with King's plans. He will soon begin recalling officers' servants and redirect convict labour to public farms. He has ordered cattle from India, and to support the weight of carcase for small settlers, he is shifting the flocks from hair to wool. He has tasked teams with working on a whaling industry and others with coal exploration. King is also supporting the emancipists, and in doing so, pushing for social inclusion. King's actions show a vivid desire to destroy the power of the Corp. Where before, his vigour was confirmed with uncomfortable displays of temper, now it is expressed in ever more violent fits of passion. I cannot help but wonder whether his health with withstand this mission.

As I watch the sunset glow gild Port Jackson, my heart is feels trapped in a thicket of personal turmoil. The sweeping reforms King has begun to introduce, though visionary and, I believe, necessary, have the potential to injure my financial aspirations. With my loyalty to Macarthur, I am promised my personal fortune, but for how long? And is the betterment of my condition worth more than the collective redemption being offered by King?

Macarthur, a man of formidable determination and loyalty to his cause, has been the architect of my prosperity. His ingenious, albeit ruthless, navigation of the Corp's assets has secured my future and offered a lifeline to many within this harsh landscape. However, his methods, marked by volatility and ambition, stand in stark opposition to King's equitable vision.

I am torn between the debt I owe to King and the bond I share with Macarthur; I find myself adrift in a sea of confusion and indecision. Prayer has offered no solution, leaving me to rely on the compass of my conscience and the call of my heart. While I could go against Macarthur, I cannot turn my back on Elizabeth, not for one second. She is more precious to me than money. Our friendship is a treasure far greater than any fortune. And so, resolute in my commitment to Macarthur, I prepare to weather the rising storm.

This choice made, albeit fraught with heartache and uncertainty, will be seen by King as the beginning of a personal conflict. I cannot she how he can take it otherwise. This rift between us will become apparent as I decline King's dinner invitation. I have been called to dine and discuss how we may bridge the chasm between his administration and the Corps. But Hugh and I, bound by blood and honour, will not attend, although the decision to absent ourselves causes me much anxiety. Our rejection of King's offer will be our declaration that we intend to stand with Macarthur.

As I grapple with the ramifications of my decision, I am reminded of the enduring promise of summer: a season of fierce light and deep shadows, of stifling air and scorching heat. I have no doubt that my future relationship with King will be true to this season. So, I offer a prayer for guidance, for the wisdom to navigate the path that lies ahead, and the strength to uphold the convictions that, even though confirmed, still cause such great concern. I beseech you Lord, that if the path I have chosen brings us into danger, protect my daughter, Sarah Ann and keep her in Your loving care.

Captain John Piper

TO THE HEART OF THE MAN

14 September 1801

As the gentle breeze of spring breathes new life and hope into Port Jackson, I find myself on a precipice of moral peril. I am waiting to be charged for participating in a man's injury, maybe death. My spirit is burdened with the weight of my actions, and the thought that they have crossed the line into disobedience to my Governor and dishonour to my office. The question that haunts my every waking moment, gnawing at me constantly, is simple yet profound: What have I done?

It is my allegiance to Macarthur that may see me come undone. I knew full well when I pledged loyalty to him, that Macarthur was a man whose resolve and ambition have often skirted the edges of insanity. However, when Patterson, our Corp's commandant and once a reliable ally, chose to align himself with King's command, Macarthur's wrath was ignited. His rage set into motion a chain of events that now threatens to engulf us all in its wake.

The discord reached a deplorable point when the private grievances of the party's wives, those keepers of the hearths and confidantes of the secrets, were drawn into the fray. Patterson's wife, in a plea for peace and restraint from Macarthur, reached out to Elizabeth by letter. Macarthur published this plea, setting the stage for Patterson to avenge his wife's honour. It was decided that there must be a duel, and Macarthur insisted I be his second. He would not allow me to decline despite the man he may kill being my dear friend.

Compelled by a loyalty to Macarthur that now seems misguided and foolish, I found myself standing beside him in the battleground. It was a role that filled me with a dread so deep it seemed to shut down my mind and leave me in a haze. The realisation that my participation could lead to the gravest of consequences left me with a sickness that seeped into my soul.

In a search for answers, I turned to Elizabeth, whose wisdom and warmth have often served as a source of sanity. Despite the constraints of her station, she possesses an uncanny insight into the machinations of men and their political processes. She counselled me with a clarity that was both comforting and stark, reminding me that the cross I had chosen was now mine to bear and that I must do so with all the courage I could muster.

The duel unfolded with a morbid tension, one at odds with the season's sparkling promise of new beginnings. This was an event that may bring about a man's end. However, it had already killed two friendships. For it was McKellar, who was chosen as Patterson's second. As we walked towards the designated spot, we could hardly look at each other; once dear companions, we were now in opposition, and the lack of ability to acknowledge each other signalled to me just how deep the pain lay. I took the toss, and it favoured Macarthur.

It also began the brutality. Macarthur, driven by motivations I can scarcely fathom, chose not the path of reconciliation but of aggression, badly wounding Patterson in the shoulder. Patterson now lies in the hospital, dangerously close to death.

My father would have been ashamed of my actions. One of my first memories of him was the serious instructions he gave about drawing a weapon; that it should only ever be done for self-defence or to remove further suffering. He had shown me how to do the latter with an injured calf once, and I could see through his stoicism to the heartbreak it caused him. He would not have agreed with any pitiful argument that honour was a legitimate excuse for taking a life. Nor would he have classed the loss of financial security as a setback significant enough to warrant this wicked act.

If the harm he caused was not enough, Macarthur then set about spitting on poor Patterson, who lay bleeding on the ground. Macarthur readily hurled insults and disdain atop Patterson's injuries. This action has left me questioning the loyalty I once pledged so freely.

How could I have sworn allegiance to a man capable of such ruthless disregard for life and honour? The turmoil that now ravages my conscience is as relentless as the spring storm sweeping across Port Jackson. I am in treacherous waters and being pushed downwards into the depths by regret and recrimination. And I know there will be severe consequences for my part in this calamitous event. King is due to return from his duties in the Hawkesbury this evening. I am sure he will be promptly advised of the duel, its participants and whether Patterson is still alive.

As I contemplate all the possible actions King may take, my thoughts turn to my daughter, Sarah Ann, now only seven and to Hugh, my dear brother, whose innocence and youth render them both particularly vulnerable to the consequences of my actions. My great hope is that I can shield them from the fallout of this grave misstep. Macarthur has offered all support necessary to see me through any criminal charges laid upon me. But I must finally find the strength to stand firm and maintain my honour. I cannot in all good conscience continue to take from a hand that is so conceited and callous.

As I grapple with the ramifications of my decision and what the daylight may bring, I offer a prayer for guidance. I also seek forgiveness for allowing myself to be caught up in such folly and for any harm that may befall Patterson and our families as a result. I am willing to take responsibility for all of it, for it is my fault.

In the tender warmth of the spring evening, I dare to hope that within this grave mistake lies a seed for redemption and the possibility of a new beginning under the providence of the Almighty. For I know, I will not receive such a compassionate hearing from King.

23 September 1801

In the silence of the night, I found myself suddenly wrenched from my home, disturbing the slumber of my housekeeper and daughter and causing much distress. I had not slept since the duel, awake and alert each night for what may come. And tonight, the action was swift. I was forcibly restrained and removed, and transported to the barracks. Beside me in a cell sits McKellar, a brick wall providing a boundary maintaining our division. I spoke with him and expressed my sorrow at how our lives have transpired and the trust that was lost. His response is not gracious, yet at least my offering has been acknowledged. The conversation was short and concluded with a stab. McKellar stated his hope that I may also get the chance to provide an apology to Patterson. I understood the connotations, given that Patterson is still gravely ill from his wound and now also battling an infection.

The cell's cold, hard walls, unyielding in their sombre embrace, seemed to mock my inner turmoil with their indifference. In the makeshift prison, the air is thick with the stench of excrement and damp earth. The dim light from outside barely penetrated the cell. Where it did, it cast long shadows that danced on the walls and taunted me with the freedom I had forgone for my sins.

Governor King met my expectations, being fierce in his condemnation of my actions. After being hauled to Government House, he vehemently expressed his disgust at how I had let Macarthur use me for his own ends. King, incessantly screaming and spitting, shared his deep concerns about Macarthur's dominating influence and warned me of the jeopardy facing my career and my brother's future. It was not the yelling that scared me, but the truth in his words. However, despite his distress and my better judgement, I found myself unable to withdraw my support for Macarthur.

When sufficient time passed for King's violent rage to ease, an earnest discourse ensued, during which he sought to appeal to a bond deeper than mere allegiance — our shared Cornish heritage. With a decidedly desperate air, he invoked the rugged perseverance of our forebears, those stalwart souls who had weathered the tempests of the Cornish coast, their spirits unbroken by the relentless sea. He spoke of the indomitable will that courses through our veins, a legacy of resilience and tenacity that has defined the sons and daughters of Cornwall for generations. Yet, even as he called upon the ties that bind us, I could not undo the one that held me to Macarthur and Elizabeth.

He stated that due to my recalcitrance, he had no alternative but to detain me, calling me a coward, amongst many other demeaning names. However, he also made clear his prime intention was not to provide punishment. King admitted it was a desperate measure to shield me from Macarthur's further manipulation and to offer me time to reflect on my future. So, I was returned to the confines of the prison. After being amongst the sumptuousness of Government House, my senses were assaulted by the acrid odour of mildew and human waste mingled with the sharp tang of iron from the bars and shackles. The rough-hewn stone beneath me offered no comfort; its cold edges were a stark reminder of the harsh reality of my existence. The faint sounds of the world beyond my cell, the murmur of voices and the occasional clatter of guards' boots only deepened my sense of isolation.

I could not fathom why I was being treated so unfairly. Why was I confined to this cell while Macarthur could still wine and dine and enjoy comfort and company under house arrest? So, I wrote to King, telling him how his reproach was hurtful and asking him to explain why my punishment was harsher than Macarthur's. His reply was curt. He simply told me to use this time to think about the answers to this question for myself.

I did think. I thought every moment about what a fool I had been. How I, too, had succumbed to the worst traits of humanity. Sitting in this prison, I wondered where I had gone wrong. Had I not learned anything on the boats about the preciousness of human life? I had seen firsthand how it can so quickly become second to greed, and judged this so harshly in others, and yet I became part of the same sin. I was burdened by a deep disappointment in myself and prayed constantly for forgiveness. I knew my intentions were noble; I needed the money to care for Sarah. However, this did not excuse reneging on the rules, bringing us all into disrepute and putting another human life in danger.

Thanks to Macarthur's contacts in the barracks, I kept receiving letters from him, making any chance of reconsideration impossible. He seemed indifferent to my plight, promising legal support if needed. However, he was also generous with veiled threats about the support that would be withdrawn if I decided to deviate from loyalty. Macarthur congratulated me for my hostility to King and the faith I had invested in him. He did not know how much it hurt or how close I came to caving in. Nor did he care.

Tormented by my choices, I reached out to Elizabeth for guidance. Again, her gentle wisdom shone through. She reminded me of the bed I'd made for myself and that there was no good in looking back. Instead, I needed to bravely face the consequences of my actions. She begged me to keep my spirits up, be cool in all I do, to not overreact, and see this through calmly. She counselled me to maintain the peace and the pride for which Pipers were known. Elizabeth was such a wonderful source of strength, but nothing could temper her husband, the tyrant.

For in a letter that followed that of Elizabeth, Macarthur made it clear that McKellar was not long for this world. He advised me to stay away from my once dear friend, telling me he was already on the chase and would not accept anyone else taking his right to revenge. I fear so gravely for McKellar and pray for his soul. I know that McKellar had done what he thought was right, and I understand the conflict of consciousness that had brought us both here. But now, his decision may be the cause of his early death.

The weight of my worry for what lies ahead is a heavy chain around my heart, compounded by my grave concern for my brother and daughter. Their faces haunt me and remind me of the potential cost of my actions — not just to my fate but to theirs as well. The possibility that my involvement in these events may have irrevocably altered the course of their lives fills me with remorse so profound it threatens to engulf me.

I seek escape from sensory deprivation by turning my mind to the spring breeze in Port Jackson. I try to imagine the wind on my face and the sense of excitement that comes with the season. Yet this respite is ended by the dread that comes with the reality I am facing, that my future may be one of shame and poverty.

My loyalty to Macarthur feels like a shackle as confining as the iron chains that bind my feet. If it was not for Elizabeth I would have flung it off before now. The conflict that rages within me, between the duty I owe to King and the allegiance I have sworn to Macarthur, leaves me adrift. I fear there may be no lamp signalling a safe shore for this situation.

I can only cling to the faint glimmer of faith that guides me. May the Lord's grace shine upon my brother, my daughter, and me, guiding us through this storm and back into the light of His benevolence.

TO THE HEART OF THE MAN

20 April 1802

As autumn gently descends upon Port Jackson, I find myself stepping into the twenty-ninth year of my life, my soul bathed in freedom. I have been found not guilty of sedition, and so reclaimed the precious gifts of my family and reputation. These blessings were secured through the support and sage counsel of Elizabeth. Under her guidance, I presented myself before the court not as a man defeated but as one whose essence is defined by honour and virtue. Following the path she had set for me, I emerged from the courthouse not merely acquitted but reborn, my status mended and ready to resume my career under God's gracious eye. I cannot help but consider how much the Corp's influence over the courts may have helped my case and how much this had played into King's mind when he sent me there. The irony is also not lost on me that the corruption I once condemned had also been the source of my salvation.

And so it is that I get to celebrate today with a birthday feast befitting an officer and spend the evening in the embrace of my family. We had hearty stews that warmed the soul and freshly baked bread, shared in a spirit of gratitude. I could not ask for a greater gift, though, than my daughter, who, at eight years of age, embodies wisdom well beyond her years. Adorned in a frock that mirrored the sky at dusk, her hair woven into braids, she was a sight of serene beauty. Her progress in her studies and the friendships she has fostered with the Macarthur children fill me with pride. However, I do notice the subtle air of displacement and caution that lingers around her and how she sometimes chooses to stand at the side. I see how she revels in time with her companions but also feels more comfortable observing this world from the periphery.

The trial that loomed over me was an ordeal that created profound introspection. In the past, I had been the one who had metered justice, deciding the fate of those afore me. Now, it was my turn to be judged, and it was a stark reminder of how fickle the winds of fate can be. The courts are a sombre assembly and yet also the crucibles within which the futures of men are forged. Standing amidst the hushed whispers of onlookers, a wave of apprehension surged within me. My stomach churned, and I hoped no one watching could see my hands shake. Yet, fortified by Elizabeth's meticulous preparations and gentle reminder of the light of goodness within me, I faced my accusers directly and honestly. She was convinced that my true nature, shining forth for all to bear witness, would shield me from condemnation, and in this, she was correct.

My release, though, has not reduced the winds of retribution that King is fanning across our colony. King's relentless pursuit of justice against Macarthur was manifested in the ordering of a court martial back in London and the dispatch of damning documents across the treacherous seas. At his behest, King had prepared extensive volumes of notes and had them made up in duplicate, each to be sent to England on a different ship. He knew the sea's dangers and would not let them overcome his obsession with holding Macarthur accountable. I have heard that these documents showed the fortune Macarthur had amassed through extortion and illegal monopolies.

The information, though, never made it to London. The first ship made it safely to England, but despite this report being heavily guarded during the voyage, when the ship docked, it was nowhere to be found. The mysterious disappearance hints at machinations only worthy of Macarthur. His influence is vast, and I am sure it played a part in this vanishing act.

I cannot be certain whether Macarthur was involved in McKellar's sad fate. McKellar was on the second ship, sent to London by King to prosecute the Court Martial against Macarthur. His ship went down, and he was never heard of again. The loss of his life to the merciless sea, a sacrifice that inadvertently secured Macarthur's liberty, fills me with a sorrow that words can scarcely convey. His unwavering sense of duty, mirroring my own, met with a fate so cruel it defies comprehension. I am continually goaded by guilt. For I was spared while McKellar's voice has been silenced. His demise, a price paid for Macarthur's freedom, is one that no man should ever bear. I wonder if King also feels the blood on his hands for sending McKellar to do his bidding.

As I reflect upon the horrific journey that has brought me to this moment, my heart overflows with gratitude for

Elizabeth, my steadfast guide through the darkest storms. Her unshakeable faith in me has cleared the path to redemption and rekindled the flame of hope. I find her compassion such a stark contrast to that of her husband, who seems so willing to place the value of his life over that of another and condemn anyone who challenges him. I understand that a father must do whatever possible to secure the prosperity of his family. However, I gravely worry when this comes at the expense of abiding by our Lord's commandments. I believe nothing good can come from those gains.

As I hold my daughter close and listen to the stories she has gathered throughout the day, I contemplate the legacy I wish to leave her; I have learnt my lessons. I pray that the impending winter will be mild and will not herald any further harm. I ask the Lord to let us live in peace for as long as possible.

14 January 1803

With Macarthur still in London, I have regained some favour with King. He has given me the command of Parramatta, an appointment that seems both a blessing and a challenge born in vengeance; I tread cautiously into my new role, unsure whether this position has been a gesture to mend bridges or a subtle reminder of my past affiliations with Macarthur. For Parramatta, while holding great potential is also a frightful place. Its current state suggests that this role could be another trial by fire, a continuation of my penance for once being labelled one of Macarthur's pawns.

This backdrop of unease is compounded by the real dangers lurking in the shadows of Parramatta's outskirts. There is a continuous threat of violence from bushrangers and a palpable tension with the natives. Settlers and convicts alike live continually in fear of what may happen next. I am called on frequently to address the audacious raids made by all manner of thieves, and their defiance of colonial authority poses a constant challenge to maintaining the peace and safety of this community. Parramatta is indeed a land of contrasts. Its promise pales under the looming threats that challenge our resolve. My role here is not just to govern but to navigate the delicate balance between law and compassion, between progress and the preservation of peace. However, I fear that I am doomed to fail. From what I have witnessed in this land to date, I suspect the prison currently under construction may be full fairly soon after completion.

In this air of anxiety, King has offered me his personal bodyguards, "The Loyal Associates". Such a proposal stirs a wariness within me. While the purpose of their presence is to ensure my safety, it's hard not to perceive it as a means for closer surveillance of me and my administration, especially during a period brimming with the risk of unrest.

The news of the Vinegar Hill rebellion in Ireland has sent ripples of concern across our community, raising the spectre of similar uprisings among the Irish convicts and settlers here in New Holland. Major Johnson, however, remains determined in his dismissal of such threats, alert to any move that might yield Parramatta's autonomy to the overarching arm of government control. Johnson ordered me to refuse King's offer, which set off a barrage of back-and-forth. With the gift of hindsight, I should have tried to distract Johnson and save his attention for bigger battles; the ceaseless correspondence did nothing but waste our precious time and wear down our fragile relationship with King even further. Although the conclusion was satisfactory. I got King to back down, dissuaded by the prospect of the administrators being seen as the prime protagonists in the settlement's destabilisation.

Amidst these trials, the joys of my personal life offer a respite from the burdens of command and remind me of all I have to be thankful for. The birthday celebration Elizabeth masterfully organised for Sarah, who recently turned nine, was truly delightful. I am endeared and indebted to her for her generosity. Despite the demands of managing the Macarthur estates in her husband's absence, Elizabeth's dedication to creating a moment of happiness for Sarah was evident in every detail of the party. The spread featured a cake, handmade by Elizabeth and her daughter, and showed the care and thoughtfulness she puts into all she does. My gifts were more practical. I had the seamstress make Sarah a new birthday dress, ensured her feet were snug in new boots, and adorned her hair with white ribbons. These gifts were simple yet filled with love and a symbol of the stability I am striving to provide this beautiful girl.

It is almost unbearable to see Elizabeth under so much stress. While she won't show it around the children, I see her in the quiet moments, her face full of tension. Her deep sighs remind me just how selfish Macarthur actually is. I know he justifies his continued jaunts as a necessity for expanding our wool exports. Yet I know the man too well to think this is his only motivation. Elizabeth does not mention it specifically, but I can sense her concern that dalliances may be occurring that could be her undoing. If this is the case, then I would have just cause to consider Macarthur not only fiendish but a fool.

As we conclude another birthday for my dear child, the concerns for Sarah's safety in this volatile environment weigh heavily on my mind. Despite Elizabeth's advice to leave the Corp, without the wage, I could not continue to give Sarah all she deserves. So, I am stuck in my current station for the foreseeable future. Still, there is so much turmoil here, so I am seeking any opportunity to move to a less threatening place. In the meantime, while I make these arrangements, I pray for the Lord to watch over my two Sarahs and keep them from harm. I also beseech the Lord to shower his grace on my family back in Maybole. Mary has written to advise that Mother has been greatly reduced in ability since my departure, and each day appears to become more fragile. Please, Lord, let her rest in your peaceful arms and restore her strength so that she may continue to serve you and maybe even, one day, see her gorgeous granddaughter.

12 June 1804

My request to be removed from Parramatta has been approved, and I thank Governor King wholeheartedly for securing the safety of my daughter. Now, the winds of change have once again swept me back to the shores of Norfolk Island. This time, it is in the company of my loyal housekeeper and my dear daughter Sarah, who has now seen ten summers. Sarah delights in the birdlife of this island and the daily spectacle of the sea's vast expanse. Sarah's adaptation to her new environment is admirable. She is making friendships at school and faring well in the lessons. The simplicity of this place has also endeared itself to my housekeeper, whose spirits have been lifted by the island's unassuming charm, a stark contrast to the chaos we left behind in Parramatta.

There are only two worries that shadow our days. The first is our distance from Elizabeth. Her absence depresses our days, filled only by her written words, which we await and consume eagerly. The second is that Norfolk Island, now under the control of Lieutenant Governor Joseph Foveaux, is far from tranquil. Foveaux's personality looms large, and his heartlessness is a grave compromise for the relative semblance of peace. It is an iron-fisted rule that now resides in Norfolk.

Foveaux suffers regularly from breathlessness and has coughing fits that leave him unable to finish his sentences. Yet he does not yield to this weakness and has not shied away from demonstrating the extent of his cruelty, especially to the convicts. I shield Sarah from the barbarity of his punishments, ensuring she does not bear witness to the public displays, fearing the indelible marks such spectacles would leave on her innocent soul. However, the Governor also does no favours for his own officers. The plight of Sergeant Sherwin, a victim of Foveaux's tyranny, serves as a harrowing reminder of the depths of his depravity. Foveaux not only stole his wife but also dragged the poor man through the distress of imprisonment and injustice. Atop all of this awful behaviour, the Governor eagerly advertises the progress he is making. Yet we all know he is merely adding superficial enhancements to the solid institutions constructed by King.

There is one unintended consequence of Foveaux's brutality, which results in some benefit for the colony. In him, we have found a common enemy, a unifying adversity, binding us all in a reluctant fellowship and strengthening the ties of comradeship. I cannot help but think the Lord has also seen fit to have me here to offer his compassion and care to those suffering from Foveaux's cruelty. My resolve to nurture trust and learn from my past misjudgements remains unshaken, and I hope to deliver the Lord's light in this darkness.

Our departure from Parramatta saved Sarah from the turmoil that everyone predicted and which eventually unfolded. I am so relieved to hear that Elizabeth escaped from the uprising. As she explained in her most recent correspondence, it was a rebellion that nearly claimed the Macarthur farm and saw her having to flee for safety by boat with her children in the dead of night. Her letters, heavy with the weight of her fears, have been a sobering reminder of the chaos we left behind and the relative blessings of being here.

From the information passed to us by Elizabeth, what is now named The Castle Hill Rebellion was fuelled by the United Irishmen, the group King was watching carefully and had warned us about. The ringleaders were well known, being Phillip Cunningham and William Johnston. Over the years, they had gathered the Irish convicts around them and, by the night of the fourth of March, had drawn together a formidable force. Their mission was clear; to establish Irish rule in the colony. Their audacious plan, inspired by the failed Emmet uprising in Dublin, aimed to seize Parramatta and Port Jackson and spur on their compatriots in the homeland.

The spark of rebellion started a raging fire of fear in the colony, and the initial band of three hundred men made swift progress. They raided the government farm buildings and seized all manner of weapons. They overpowered the constables and overseers and raided each farm on their way to Parramatta, where they gathered more supplies and spirits and enlarged their gang. Upon arrival at Constitution Hill, Cunningham was elected King of the Australian Empire, and his followers declared the area New Ireland.

These men, though, could not hold the empire against martial law and the swift mobilisation of the military. Through the dead of night, King bolstered the defences of Parramatta, confining the rebels to the west, and then he trapped them with forces from the other side. He quashed the uprising with a ruthless efficiency that left fifteen men dead, although there would have been much more blood spilt if Major Johnston had not cautioned his men to show temperance. Over the coming days, over two hundred rebels were brought in to receive their punishment. King's stipulations were set to quell any future dissent. He had nine executed, and seven were dealt the sentence of five hundred lashes, which would have left them close to death. Others were sent to chain gangs, the coal mines or Norfolk Island on good behaviour orders. Some of these men have already arrived and provided many more details about this fateful event. Those able to prove they were coerced were pardoned and ordered to return to their employment, surely relieved that they did not meet a more disastrous end.

Elizabeth's recount of the revolt's suppression, a grim narrative of violence and retribution, reinforces my gratitude that we were spared from witnessing such horrors firsthand. Yet, this gratitude is tinged with the realisation of Foveaux's own propensity for ruthlessness. This dilemma has me contemplating a refuge elsewhere, and I am in the midst of enquiring into the fledging settlement in Van Diemen's Land. Perhaps joining this new colony, at its genesis, will allow me to better influence the leadership and build a society founded on compassion and Christian values.

4 October 1804

Today's dawn brought with it a new chapter, not just for myself and my dear Sarah but for the entire community that cradles us. Foveaux's darkness has receded back to England. Apparently, the island is irksome to Foveaux's asthma, and a sea voyage is deemed to be the solution to ease the condition. And, In His infinite wisdom, the Almighty has steered my fate to the helm of this colony. I am now the administrator of Norfolk Island. It appears King still holds me in good stead, adding Lieutenant Governor to my mantle. It is a title I will not hold for long as the closure of this penal settlement looms closer. Yet, as we seek to close down this island, I discern a promise of a potential new beginning for us in Van Diemen's Land. This fledgling state whispers promises of a fresh start, a chance to sow seeds of prosperity on untainted ground.

I cannot help but think how the transition of seasons mirrors the transition of governance. As the island basks in the increasing warmth of spring, its blossoms unfurling, my heart has also opened with a new sense of purpose. The mandate to dismantle this colony, though a decree from distant shores, is a canvas upon which I yearn to paint a legacy of compassion and equity. Freed from the yoke of tyranny that once choked the life from this land, I now wield the power to steer our course towards a horizon bright with the promise of dignity and respect for all souls under my care.

My first action was to visit the prison, and my inaugural order was to treat all prisoners with the humanity they deserve. While this command came from my mouth, it was merely transferred through me from God. It was also far more than an instruction. It was a vow made before God and man to right the wrongs inflicted under Foveaux's reign. No one knows these wrongs more intimately than Holt, whose only sin was to be born Irish in a time of suspicion and strife. I personally spoke with Holt, who Foveaux singled out as a scapegoat, always metering out sadistic treatment to send signals to the other Irish prisoners. I saw his merciless torture regularly. Every day since my return swore that if ever given the chance, I would make it right. Today, thank the Lord, I got my chance. The liberation of Holt from his undeserved chains is but the first step back onto a path of rectitude.

As the oppressive air from Foveaux dissipates, a newfound spirit of camaraderie takes root among us. The communal sigh of relief, palpable in the spring air, breathes life into the very earth we till, nurturing a sense of solidarity. Perhaps it is too vain to credit this transformation to my influence alone. Still, I cannot help but hope that my actions have kindled a flame of optimism and hope in people's hearts.

In recognition of the hard truth that sustenance quells discontent more effectively than any decree, I have doubled the flour ration. It is a move that I pray will ease the gnawing hunger that has long been our constant companion. Moreover, the promise of pardons for those who have demonstrated loyalty and good conduct is not merely a gesture of goodwill but a covenant of trust—a trust in the potential for redemption and the power of second chances.

My resolve to fortify our supply lines and to refine the use of convict labour speaks not to a desire for efficiency alone but to a commitment to the humane treatment of those in our charge. I desperately hope these reforms will meld prosperity with compassion, extol the dignity of every soul and lay the groundwork for a community rooted in mutual respect and shared aspirations.

As I pen these words, the crisp sea air fills my lungs, expanding a sense of hope and responsibility. I am reminded of the many voyages I have taken where I was prevented from being of service to those who were suffering. Today, I swear that for however long I may be honoured with this post, I will do all I can to compensate for these missed opportunities. It is my deepest prayer that my stewardship of this land, in these pivotal months, will be looked upon with favour by God and man alike. And may Sarah, my light and my love, finally witness me leading with a heart full of generosity and grace. May I teach her that true wealth is garnered not from the coffers of commerce but from the riches of a compassionate spirit.

The Irish rebel convict, Joseph Holt, declared, "the new Governor had the good will and respect of everyone, for he had always conducted himself as a Christian and a gentleman."

14 November 1804

As the days become increasingly bright and warm, my soul becomes more tightly ensnared in the whirlwind of duties involved in overseeing this island. Each day, I retire completely drained from the weight of responsibility that now rests upon my shoulders. The earlier rising sun makes for longer days; each hour is needed to attend to the enormous tasks ahead. In the past weeks since I assumed command, the dual spectres of excitement and exhaustion have become my constant companions. Mending the torn fabric of trust that Foveaux's reign of terror rent on our small community — is a monumental undertaking. Yet, beneath my weary bones lies a firm and fundamental belief that my work is of the utmost importance, a sacred duty to which I have been called.

Though blessed with the natural bounty of spring, our island bears the scars of neglect and tyranny. The infrastructure, vital to our survival and prosperity, languishes in disrepair. The mills stand silent, their grindstones worn to nubs, the saws succumbed to rust, and an absence of skilled hands. The lack of a master carpenter's expertise curtails our ambitions. Yet, there is a greater trial - the education and care of the island's forsaken children — those young souls cast adrift in a sea of illiteracy and neglect. There are now over two hundred bastard children, almost one-fifth of our entire population, and many run wild with no form of discipline or oversight. Establishing schooling and pastoral care for these innocents consumes not just the daylight hours but every essence of my energy and ingenuity.

The jail, a dark heart within our midst, demands much of my attention. The orders I provide to the head jailer, Robert Jones, are my attempt to peel back the layers of a regime that saw the lash become a much-overused weapon. Foveaux's legacy, etched in the stone of the buildings and in the flesh of the convicts, shows the virility of his belief in punishment over rehabilitation. I have heard the horrific stories of how, when tools failed, a day's labour turned to torture. Those who dared voice their suffering were subsequently flogged. Some convicts were driven to despair and oftentimes committed more crimes in the hopes of being sent to Port Jackson. These tales tell of a devilish darkness that I am determined to dispel.

I have also met with Joseph Mansbury, a man so often the recipient of the lash that his back appeared bare of flesh, and his collar bones had become like two ivory polished horns. The thought of the flogger resorting to the soles of his feet for further punishment leaves me feeling ill. The count book shows he received over two thousand lashes in three years, a trial that would have killed a lesser man. Such punishment killed Thomas Carpenter, and I can see the sadness in Jones' eyes when we share the story of his desired escape. Carpenter hit an officer, hoping that he would be sent back to Port Jackson to obtain justice and thus escape from Foveaux's evils. But Foveaux got to him first. The first two hundred and fifty lashes killed him. He died of heart failure and never got to see the friends in Port Jackson that he cherished or the chance of justice.

Instead, he died with the callous flogger's chanting in his ears - "Another half-pound, mate, off the beggar's ribs." He would have left this earth with the vision of a man standing above him, covered in flesh from the day's victims and Foveaux wickedly wheezing, "How do you like it?" It was only with his death that he avoided the fate of so many others, who, after their floggings, were then ordered to put their coats back on and go immediately back to work.

Sentences of "feelers", a taste of two hundred lashes were commonplace. The barbaric "salty back" treatment stands as a stark reminder of the inhumanity that I seek to eradicate. The tightening of leg irons each month to pinch the flesh, the isolation in black cells, and the water pits designed to instil fear of drowning are horrors that I cannot allow to persist under my command.

In the quietude that often blankets our evenings, my conversations with Thomas Hibbins, the deputy judge advocate, serve as a tremendous source of support. He stood against Foveaux's draconian measures, his compassion for the convicts a stark contrast to the cold legalism that often pervaded our discourse under the previous Governor. He staunchly believes in the illegality of Foveaux's methods, particularly the flagrant disregard for due process. We discussed the disgraceful treatment of Wolloghan and McClean—two souls unceremoniously executed under the guise of quelling dissent. The flambeaux-lit execution, devoid of trial or testimony, was an example of nothing less than tyranny.

As expected, the subsequent investigation was a sham, washing Foveaux clean of wrongdoing. Instead of being punished, he was praised and promoted by his English masters, elevating him in rank rather than holding him to account. This unreasonable and unjust outcome only served to further ignite the embers of discontent among us. It is this smouldering anger, born of injustice and cruelty, that I now seek to quench with the waters of empathy. However, the memory of past atrocities looms large and creates a massive mountain that I must move.

The horrors of Foveaux's reign were made ever more clear during today's excitement. A ship was sighted in the distance and believed to be a fleet of invaders seeking to overthrow our island. While we hurriedly prepared for our defence it was confirmed the fleet was actually a convoy of Chinese traders escorted by the French warship L'Athenienne. The relief made us all laugh and brought a moment of levity, with us wondering just how we would secure the island with the only ammunition at hand being broken bottles. However, this moment of mirth was quickly overshadowed by the discovery of Foveaux's final, cruel order: the mass execution of prisoners in the event of an invasion. The prison guards were readying to follow through on the previous plan, and it was only for the swift action taken by one of the officers that called it to my attention. I thank God that the news got to me in time and that I was able to prevent the slaughter. My soul has never before felt so troubled.

As I retire each evening to dine with my beloved Sarah, her presence reminds me of the purity and innocence I fight to protect. Our conversations, often punctuated by the distant memories of Elizabeth's correspondence, are islands of peace in the stormy seas of governance. The challenges ahead are numerous, and the path is fraught with obstacles, but I remain undaunted. For within me burns a flame fuelled by the conviction that my work here is not just for the benefit of those under my command but for the legacy we leave for future generations.

My prayers each night are for the strength to carry on, to right the wrongs of the past, and to guide our community towards a future where dignity, respect, and compassion are the cornerstones upon which we build. May the Lord grant me the fortitude to continue this vital work, for in the healing of others, I find the salve for my own weary soul.

TO THE HEART OF THE MAN

10 January 1805

As the new year unfolds, our community is cradled in the arms of stifling summer and awash with the ever-increasing presence of sweat. We are all heavy, somewhat hard-hearted, and short-tempered from the heat. We long for the late afternoon sea breeze and the end of the day to gain rest from the hard work. This evening, we had another cause to celebrate: the coming of Sarah's eleventh year. Here on Norfolk Island, it is a milestone not marked not by grandeur but by the simplicity of love and nature's bounty.

The birthday table, though modest in comparison to those orchestrated by Elizabeth, was adorned with a woven basket, brimming with the island's most splendid flora — oleander, big creeper, tea tree, hibiscus, and popwood. The air was perfumed with their intoxicating scents, uplifting all our spirits. This gift, received with unparalleled joy by Sarah, was a testament to the generosity she shows to the simplest of gestures.

Our feast was graced by a cake made possible by the recent increase in flour rations. Though it lacked the exuberance of Elizabeth's creations, it symbolised our love for this dear girl and our great wishes for her future. The meal was true to the life on this island. There was freshly baked bread that filled the air with its comforting aroma, a stew of local vegetables and a fish caught by the settlers, its flavour enhanced by the herbs grown in our own gardens. The laughter and conversation that accompanied the meal were as nourishing to our souls as the food was to our bodies.

In Sarah, I see not just the joy of youth but the embodiment of the hope and potential that lies within our island community. Her compassionate nature, dedication to the Church, and tender care for the younger children are such sources of pride. I wish that one day soon, she shall extend her nurturing to many siblings. First, though, I must find myself a wife, but with all the work here to do, that is unlikely to eventuate within the foreseeable future.

The heaviness of the season has also been matched by a sinking feeling in my heart. I strive to do the best for the people here and the powers back in Port Jackson. However, recently, I have received a reprimand from Governor King. He has taken a disliking to the communal gatherings I've initiated, particularly the Thursday night entertainments. I have instituted these in an effort to restore the weary spirits of our people and bring us together in an atmosphere of support. Far from the debauchery King imagines, these evenings of companionship and revelry are vital oases of joy in the desert of our exile. Music, storytelling, and dance have become our salves, healing the wounds inflicted by years of hardship. In defiance of King's misgivings, I maintain that these gatherings are the essence of our rebirth and a necessary celebration of our humanity.

I reject his notion that these behaviours signal a 'relaxed' approach to my leadership. I assert they are actually required to restore the human spirit after years of horrendous rule. I have also dismissed his accusations that they give me cause to cavort with the local women. They are not cavortings; they are congenialities, always conducted with the greatest regard and respect.

I suspect this censure is a result of the stress King is facing. The spectre of Macarthur's return looms large, and undoubtedly, King is preparing himself for the conflicts that will again ensnare his life. King's anxiety manifests as criticism of my governance, likely intended to remind me of my place. No reminder is necessary, for I am more than happy to stay away from the fray and continue my important work here on the island. My tenure on Norfolk Island, marked by both trials and triumphs, is a journey I wish to continue. It offers a sanctuary from the storms that rage beyond our shores. Our days here are difficult, but not more so than the dilemma I faced during the duel. I have a clear path forward here and do not wish to have it waylaid.

Macarthur's ongoing ambitions are clear evidence of his tenacity, but they also threaten to unsettle the fragile balance in Port Jackson. Elizabeth has advised him to seek claim over the Cowpastures, a land of rich soil and vital waters, and use this to expand his private holdings. As King grapples with the implications of Macarthur's pursuits, I find myself caught in the crossfire of their discord. However, here I am at a distance from both men and with the delays in the post, there is little practical support I can offer by letter.

As I navigate the complexities of leadership and the intricacies of colonial politics, I am resolute in my focus on the tasks at hand — nurturing our community, stewardship of our land, and safeguarding our collective spirit. I pray that the Lord may see fit to keep me here as long as possible and out of harm's way. May the return of Macarthur bring not strife but solace to Elizabeth and her children, and may our efforts on this island be richly rewarded.

"The convicts, who were deeply impressed with the grateful sense of what they owe to your kindness, respectfully entreat you to accept their unfeigned thanks for the humane and indulgent treatment, they have experienced under your command. They took the liberty of expressing their ardent wishes for your happiness and welfare and with your benevolent disposition you may ever possess the power of doing good." ~ *Letter from two convicts Richard Day and Edward O'Hara to John Piper 22 February 1805.*

2 February 1806

Today, I am engulfed in the extremes of emotion, pulled between events that, on the one hand, celebrate the very essence of creation and another that seem to mock its very existence. I have become aware that a young girl named Elizabeth Eddington, aged fourteen, is claiming to carry my child. In truth, I have heard rumours that I may not have been the only one in the colony she enchanted. Still, I cannot contest the fact that there is a chance it is mine. Neither would I put her family through the turmoil of making assertions against her. I will own my actions and do what I can to make this situation conducive for the child's good fortune, for they should not pay for their parents' failings.

Indeed, there is part of my heart that exalts at the thought of providing Sarah with siblings, and yet it is also heavy with a complex mix of guilt and responsibility. My daughter, Sarah, has greeted the news with a similar swirl of confusion, at one point looking excited and, shortly after, aghast. She harbours deep reservations about Elizabeth's situation, troubled by the implications of Elizabeth being a single mother within this society and the prospect of welcoming a stranger's child into our family dynamics.

Amidst these revelations, I am resolved to care for and respect Elizabeth and our forthcoming child. I am inspired by my daughter's resilience and prudence amid complex situations. As we move forward, I am determined to navigate this challenging path with dignity and hope that this will bring no shame upon Sarah, Elizabeth or my future children. I am intent that the Lord's love remains at the core of our family's journey. I know it is possible to tread this path with integrity. My daughter, now by my side, is clear evidence that such an outcome can exist.

I have also heard from Mrs Marsden, whose husband has been very capably managing my estates in my absence. My darling horse Kitty is now in foal. This offspring brings me such great hope. It is more than the simple continuation of her line—it whispers of a legacy I may yet cultivate within the colony. Here, I may have found the land where I can create a lineage, a stable of fine horses, and a breed that might one day become synonymous with the Piper name.

Alongside the news of this new life about to unfold, I find myself grappling with a notice that heralds its destruction. The directive has come, decreeing the dissolution of the Norfolk Island colony. With a heart laden with sorrow, I am to orchestrate the unravelling of a community that has, against all odds, started to recover under my stewardship. The despair that grips me is but a reflection of the heartache that is felt by all.

The people of this island, who have toiled with unwavering resolve, now will have the fruits of their labours prised from their worn fingers. Their farms, the very embodiments of their hopes and dreams, businesses, and homes—constructed with the sweat of their brows and the strength of their backs — are to be relinquished. The ledger of assets I am preparing is a cold and heartless record of their efforts. And yet I am determined that it serves as some consolation as they seek to rebuild their lives in the unfamiliar terrains of Van Diemen's Land. I am committed to securing pardons and ensuring fair compensation for the land and stock of my people. For I witness their anguish daily. Farmers come to me with tears etching furrows deeper than those in their soil, unwilling to leave all that they have worked so hard to nurture. Wives beseech me to guide their husbands through the despair of knowing their creations will be left to decay.

The command to dismantle our community is not born of malice but of a grim pragmatism dictated by distant authorities. Our existence here has been deemed to be unsustainable and too costly. These judgements are easy to make for those who have never set foot on our soil. Yet, knowing the rationale does little to temper the heartbreak or to soothe the sense of betrayal. For the last four months, I have endeavoured to sow seeds of hope and resilience within this community. Now, I find myself the harbinger of its demise.

My concern for the wellbeing of these individuals, who have weathered storms made by both God and man, is paramount.

In this hour of despair, I turn to the Almighty, beseeching His guidance and strength. May He grant me the fortitude to navigate this sorrow and embody the same grace and benevolence He has shown unto His flock. I pray that the resilience that has defined our time on this island will continue as we face the daunting prospect of starting anew. My prayers also turn to Elizabeth, that she will be kept safe during her pregnancy and that the Lord will see fit to bring a healthy child into this world. If He grants this prayer, I promise to do all I can to have it grow into a generous servant of His word.

20 April 1806

As I mark the passage of my thirty-second on this earth, there is no cause for celebration. The news reached me like a bitter wind that on the ninth day of February, my beloved mother departed from this world. This weighs heavy on my soul, the sorrow adding to the already oppressive duty of dismantling our settlement. It also makes the impending arrival of new life from Elizabeth feel excruciating.

The thought haunts me, gnawing at the edges of my weary mind that perhaps it was a broken heart that claimed my mother. I did not tell her of my circumstance, but maybe through Hugh, she learnt of my failings and the scandal of fathering two children out of wedlock. The bitter realisation that she never embraced her granddaughter Sarah nor witnessed the bond that I am certain would have flourished between them is a torment that words scarce can convey. Sarah, too, is engulfed in grief, yearning for the connection to her extended family that now will never be. Though she finds support in the friendships forged with the elder settlers, the absence of her grandmother is a pain that can never be fully consoled.

I am left to imagine the funeral of my mother, my mind wandering to the rugged landscapes of rural Scotland, envisioning the solemn procession that would have accompanied her casket to the final resting place. There would have been stark simplicity, the community coming together in a display of unity and support. I picture the small stone church, standing resolute against the Scottish moors, its doors open to receive one of its own for the last time. The mournful melodies of traditional dirges carried on the wind would have mingled with the whispered prayers of those gathered. The burial would have been a quiet affair, surrounded by the sobs of her children and grandchildren. She would have been laid to rest beneath the verdant embrace of the land she called home, her spirit released to the heavens amidst the recitation of scripture and the shared memories of a life fully lived.

In my darkest moments, when the light of fortitude flickers and threatens to extinguish, I find myself wrestling with a rough sea of emotions. The belief that my mother now rests in the Lord's embrace is a small comfort against the tide of anger and despair that consumes me. For in taking her from this world, it feels as though He has exacted a cruel toll, one that leaves me bereft and questioning the very foundations of my faith. I sit here in despair, gazing into the abyss of anguish, and I confess, with a heart laden with grief, that I now harbour a hatred for the Almighty.

4 May 1806

In the quiet stirrings of early May, under the ever-increasingly brisk breezes that swirl around the island, our household finds itself on the verge of an astounding adjustment. Sarah, my honourable housekeeper, has been graced with the miracle of life stirring within her – something we all thought impossible given her age.

Her excitement at the contemplation of being a mother, a yearning I believe she has always had, is being tempered with a stoic grace. She is also cognisant that Elizabeth Eddington's child, another of my own, will soon be born, and so she is not alone in bearing an heir. Despite the complexity cast by these circumstances, Sarah's response has been nothing short of magnanimous, her surprise at her own fertility at the age of forty-five tinged with a quiet acceptance of the life we cannot share through marriage.

My daughter, ever optimistic, embraces the prospect of Sarah's child with open arms, heralding it as a joy and another example of the enduring bonds that define our unconventional family. Yet, amidst our anticipation, a veil of concern lingers over Sarah's wellbeing. There are dual challenges ahead; her advanced age and the island's limited medical provisions. In recognising her invaluable role in our lives, I resolve to ensure her comfort and security. Sarah, who has been both guardian and guide to my daughter and myself, shall want for nothing. We all wait with bated breath for the birth and pray repeatedly that all will be well.

24 August 1806

As the wheel of time turns, so too do the fortunes of my friends. In June of last year, Macarthur, a figure as divisive as he is driven, made a triumphant return to Port Jackson. I have heard how he arrived aboard a vessel he aptly named the Argo, a nod to the audacious spirit of mythological adventurers. His entrance was made all the more striking by a figurehead of a sheep adorning the bow, as much a declaration of his ambitions as it was a of his arrogance. Accompanied by five rams and a single ewe, he has made his first moves towards his vision; an empire woven in wool. He has also, unfortunately, forecast further battles with King over the endowment of land.

My recent correspondences from Macarthur have been a steady stream of entreaties and veiled provocations, each letter an attempt to draw me into the orbit of his discontent with Governor King. Yet I find peace away from the politics and delight in the detachment that Norfolk Island affords, allowing me to observe from afar the drama that seems to follow Macarthur relentlessly. I can resist writing too regularly, allowing things to unfold without my involvement.

I am glad to hear that King will soon retire from the post of Governor, for I am sure it has done much damage to his health. His replacement is to be William Bligh, which may be seen as either a blessing or a curse for the colony. I have heard from many sources of Bligh's strict obeyance of orders at the expense of empathy and how, in the past, this has put him on the path of mistrust, rebellion and mutiny. I pray that he may see fit to continue King's legacy and have due regard for the people, for they have suffered enough to endure another tyrant and would be more than willing to create unrest to usurp one.

For while Macarthur would have my head if he heard me say this, King's contributions to the colony have been positive. Under his stewardship, Port Jackson and Norfolk Island witnessed stability grow from the seeds of his labours. King's legacy has been woven into the fabric of our community, and into the soils with the sustainable agriculture practices that provided food for all. Fair trade, while egregious to us who had profited from its opposite, was just, leading to a more equitable distribution of resources. Under his guidance, buildings were erected that served functional purposes and instilled a sense of permanence and progress. His efforts to foster relations with the indigenous populations also opened avenues for a more harmonious coexistence. Yes, while I have had my share of conflict with King, I consider him a fair and successful administrator, and one that I seek to mirror in my own management.

As there is great change afoot back in Port Jackson, there is also an alteration in my personal circumstances. On the sixteenth of August, amidst conditions that would test the strongest among us, Elizabeth brought forth a baby boy, my first son, to be named John after me. I am so greatly relieved knowing that Elizabeth and the child have emerged from this ordeal unscathed, though it does little to ease the ache of being a father in name only.

The decision of her parents to escort her back to Port Jackson, while prudent, is also hurtful. John is my son, my first son, and should be known to his father and given the chance to follow in his footsteps. I should have the chance to shape him as a man and teach him all that I know. This is my duty, but more than that, it would be my honour to protect and guide my son through the wilds of this new world. However, Elizabeth's father knows that I cannot marry one of her station and so she would be left here as a shameful single mother. At least on the mainland, she may have the chance to be taken in as a concubine and have our son cared for in a fortunate home. It tears at my heart thinking about this future for her and my son, and yet I see here, with my two Sarahs, how it could end well.

I have provided for the passage of her family and a tidy sum for my son's care. With these funds I seek not absolution but to fulfil a duty that honour and decency demand. It is a gesture, however inadequate, towards a son whose life will unfold far from my guiding hand.

In the quiet hours of the night, when the ghosts of my decisions come to haunt me, I find myself wrestling with a profound sense of loss — not just for the son I cannot claim but for the mother who has departed this world. Yet, even as despair threatens to cloud my vision, I still feel a spark of faith within me. The anger I have held onto for several months is subsiding to be replaced with due regard for divine decisions. The Lord, in His infinite wisdom, has called her to His side, and in this, I must seek solace.

28 November 1806

As the dusk settles upon our home, it brings with it a tale of tremendous endurance. Sarah, my courageous companion has brought forth into this world a daughter whom we have named Mary Ann. The ordeal of her birth was a saga, stretching over more than one day and delivering pain that filled this space with fearsome screams. I found myself at times gravely worried for Sarah's wellbeing, fearing that her body may be broken by the birth or that exhaustion might cause her end. While I was not privy to the happenings within the chamber, my daughter, who witnessed the birth, explained to me how the wise and well-skilled midwives applied compresses, murmured words of encouragement, and guided her through the tempest of her labour.

Now, tiny Mary Ann slumbers, and Sara lies lethargic but alive. My daughter, with a tenderness that belies her years, has assumed the mantle of caregiver, affording Sarah the respite she so desperately needs to mend the wear wrought upon her body and spirit. This woman has gone through so much for our family, and although the bonds of matrimony elude us, I will do all that is right by Sarah and our child. Mary Ann shall be baptised under my name, a symbol of my pledge to shelter and nurture them both within the sanctity of our home. I pray for their health and happiness and entreat the Heavens to find a way, somehow, to preserve this newly formed family. For even though it is not recognised by law, it feels right and true.

01 April 1807

Mid-autumn is upon us, and over the past months, our household has witnessed many milestones. In January, we celebrated a momentous occasion, marking Sarah's passage into her thirteenth year. This entrance into maturity now heralds new responsibilities for me as her father. The time has come to contemplate her future, to seek out a companion who embodies both strength of character and the promise of prosperity, a union that will ensure her place in a world that often demands much more than it gives.

The Easter just past was a truly heart-warming and memorable occasion. Our observance of Easter Sunday began at dawn with a service that paid due homage to the sacred traditions we hold dear. The hymns, carried on the brisk morning air, spoke of resurrection and hope, their melodies mixing with the distant crash of waves against the shore. Following the service, we shared a communal meal, a feast of bread baked with the last of the summer's wheat, stews enriched with the hearty root vegetables of autumn, and sweet pies that used all of our sugar rations for the month.

As we broke bread and shared stories, the children of our community engaged in games of hide-and-seek among the trees. In this moment, away from the turmoil and uncertainties of the wider world, we found joy in each other and contentment in the cycle of the seasons.

Mary Ann, now four months cradled in the passage of time, has become a daily reminder of the miraculous unfurling of life. Each day with her brings new wonders — the first stirrings of recognition in her eyes, the spontaneous smiles that light up her face, and the babbling that fills our home is the music of sheer joy. I see her growth as a silent hymn to the magic of creation, a reminder of the divine craftsmanship at play in the world around and within us.

Yet, just as I am buoyed by this beautiful baby's presence, I am also preparing myself to see her and her mother away. Tomorrow, I will bid farewell to Sarah, my housekeeper, and Mary Ann as they embark on a journey to Port Jackson for the baby's baptism. I will follow them promptly. However, while I will return to continue my work on the island, Sarah and Mary Ann will remain on the mainland. Thanks to Elizabeth's foresight, Sarah enters Port Jackson not as an evacuee from the doomed Norfolk Island colony but with the dignity of one coming of her own accord. Elizabeth has secured Sarah's employment in Port Jackson and is personally assured that both mother and child will be afforded due care and consideration.

The prospect of being separated from Sarah and Mary Ann creates chaos within me. Sarah has been beside me as a housekeeper and supporter for what feels like a lifetime, and I know I could not find a companion more capable and constant. How I will fare without them close, I do not know. It may only be the vast effort required here that will provide a sufficient distraction from this despair. It is a hard cross to bear, but at least in Port Jackson, Sarah and Mary Ann will be under the watchful eye of Elizabeth. If they were to be sent to Van Diemen's land, they would be surrounded by strangers.

In their absence, my elder daughter's temporary guardianship falls to another, a placeholder until we can plan our future with further confidence. Whether our path leads back to Port Jackson or ventures towards Van Diemen's Land remains a question cloaked in uncertainty. Elizabeth's counsel will be sought, albeit with a cautionary distance from her husband. Macarthur continues his requests for me to join him in the wool trade, but I cannot see any way in which I can trust this man with my future or that of my family.

Besides, at least for the short term, I am dedicated to serving this island and its people. I have seen fit to build upon the foundation that Governor King established and have recently reduced the colony's reliance on government rations to a mere thirty-two per cent and significantly diminished our debt. King's efforts, and those of his wife, in advocating for the potential of Norfolk Island, underscore a belief in the slow yet steady cultivation of sustainable prosperity — a belief tragically overlooked by his superiors in England but which could have prevented the island's premature abandonment.

As I consider my imminent journey to Port Jackson, I am filled with both anticipation and anxiety. The prospect of reuniting with Elizabeth Macarthur, to witness firsthand the growth of her family and to receive her wise counsel, fills my heart with gladness. However, the thought of encountering her husband, now embroiled in escalating confrontations with Governor Bligh, brings me no joy. Bligh has done much to stir Macarthur, banning the trade in rum, threatening to withdraw Macarthur's leases and demolishing Macarthur's buildings on government land to make way for public gardens. None of these actions bode well for a peaceful future. From what I can tell from my regular correspondence, it is only breeding an air of trepidation. I pray that no innocent people will get caught up in their conflict and any damage done to the governance of the colony will be readily rectified. Dear Lord, please send both of these brutal men some of your wisdom.

24 December 1807

On this sacred eve, as the air hung heavy with the weight of humidity and reverence, and as the community gathered for the evening service, I was graced with the sight of a girl who seemed more divine than human. As the congregation raised their voices in prayer and amid the flickering candlelight, I beheld Mary Ann.

I had known her name from the ledgers used in managing the island's affairs. Sometimes, I had seen her from a distance, but her father kept her far away. Now, she was no longer a child but a woman of grace and generosity, and her father had recognised the time was right for her to be released into society. As she sang, my heart leapt. Her father, once shackled by the chains of convict life but now a free man, was wise to keep her in close quarters, for she is a jewel that so many would seek to claim. Her dark hair framed her face like the night frames the moon, and her eyes, deep and fathomless, reflected a soul both kind and resolute. When our gazes met, a silent covenant was forged. I knew, with a certainty that defied reason, that my life was irrevocably altered. I had no choice but to request the company of Mary Ann and her father on the morrow for tea, an invitation extended with a heart full of hope and a spirit buoyed by the prospect of kinship.

Back in Port Jackson, Sarah and my beloved daughter have now settled within their new sanctuary, thanks to the generous efforts of Elizabeth. Her acumen has secured Sarah a position of respect, a household over which she may preside with the dignity she so richly deserves and a place where Mary Ann will be well cared for. The relief that accompanies this knowledge is immense, but it cannot fill the hole in my life that is made by their absence. I know in my heart that the circumstances we find ourselves in are not uncommon. This island, as is Port Jackson, is teeming with infants who have not been conceived in the bonds of matrimony. And yet, I cannot help but turn my mind to my mother and what her opinion of me would be. There are now three children that I have caused to be called bastards and are termed illegitimate. Nevertheless, we must face a reality in these colonies, which, to my credit, I did attempt to deny and run from. I will no longer ignore the responsibility that comes with this reality, nor shy away from sense, and instead deal with these situations with dignity.

There is increasingly disturbing news about the turbulent currents stirring in Port Jackson. The conflict between Governor Bligh and Macarthur is intensifying with a ferocity that bodes ill for all who are caught within its wake. Bligh's resolve to quell the illicit production of spirits has sparked a confrontation where the courtroom has become the battleground for a war, one waged with the weapons of law and order. Bligh has now realised the extent to which the Corp runs the courts. The trial he instigated against Macarthur has backfired upon him, and he has now been branded a ruthless Governor. The impounding of Macarthur's schooner and the dismantling of his fences — these acts of defiance from Bligh are met with equal obstinacy from Macarthur. Bligh has continued to escalate the battle, accusing Macarthur of treason. With this claim he has sounded a clarion call to the Corp that I am sure will be the start of further turmoil. I have no doubt that Macarthur will rally the Corp around him to fight these serious charges and use this as a convenient excuse to increase the stakes even further. I have grave concerns about where this battle of wills may end.

As I retire to my quarters this evening, my prayers are for the safety of all those embroiled in this power struggle — for Elizabeth, for Sarah, for little Mary Ann, and for the soul of Port Jackson itself. I implore providence to shield them and entrust our fates to the unwavering grace of the Almighty. And I seek the blessings of the Lord for my meeting with Mary Ann and her father tomorrow. I pray that He may grant my wish to be with her in whatever capacity is possible.

TO THE HEART OF THE MAN

18 March 1808

As the days march forward, so does the tide of events that shape our distant colony. The waves bring forth news of revolution from the mainland, delivered through the fragmented accounts of friends embroiled in the thick of it — alerting me to Governor Bligh's arrest and the subsequent upheaval that has shaken the foundations of Port Jackson.

Tales of the turmoil have arrived in hastily penned and often breathless letters from my colleagues in Port Jackson. The pages, folded and sealed with urgency, speak of what they have called the Rum Rebellion. This name does not do justice to the gravity of the events that transpired in January.

Through the ink-stained lines on the letters, I have gleaned the nature of the insurrection. Once the unchallenged authority in New South Wales, Governor William Bligh has found his reign abruptly severed by the very hands that once saluted him. The Corps were driven to mutiny by what they perceived as Bligh's oppressive edicts. His stringent regulation of the rum trade and the personal vendetta against Macarthur pushed them to take the ultimate of actions, to cast aside their oaths to crown and command.

I have read the accounts of the fateful day when Major George Johnston, propelled by the Corps and incited by the rum traders, stormed Government House. They describe a scene that would have been almost comical were it not for the stark reality of its consequences. The once formidable Governor Bligh was found hidden beneath a bed; his governance toppled without a single shot fired.

The echoes of this power struggle resonate deeply as I learn of the Corps' swift establishment of a military government with Major Johnston at its helm. Friends speak of a peculiar stillness that has since descended upon Port Jackson — a quietude born from the barrel of a gun, fragile and fraught with the potential for fracture. Major George Johnston, in his missives, proclaims a return to tranquillity, yet I harbour no illusions of such peace enduring. With Macarthur's influence still cast over the colony and the impending arrival of a new governor, I foresee but a temporary lull in the storm.

The accounts of the rebellion are as varied as the men who recount them. Still, it is Elizabeth's correspondence that I hold in the highest regard. Through her eyes, I see the rebellion not as a popular uprising but as a coup d'état, orchestrated by the Corps with Machiavellian precision, not to liberate but to entrench their own power. Her words paint a picture of officers embroiled in ugly conflict, their unity dissolving into mistrust and hatred as soon as their common foe was vanquished. It is a spectacle that she assures would have roused my utmost contempt, and her counsel to Macarthur echoes with a forewarning that the greatest threat they may face comes from within their own ranks.

It is a strange sensation to be both distant and yet so intimately connected to these upheavals. While the seas separating Norfolk Island from the mainland offer a buffer from the immediate impact of such events, the reverberations are felt, stirring the waters surrounding us. The letters from my colleagues are a lifeline, pulling me into the eye of a storm that I observe from afar yet which threatens to draw me into its vortex upon my return.

In the midst of this chaos, our Lord has seen fit to bestow upon me a grace of the purest form. Mary Ann, my heart's companion, carries our first child — a blessing conceived in the bloom of our newfound unity. At seventeen, she stands at the threshold of motherhood, her countenance one of strength. Each day, her presence in our household transcends the ordinary. She brings the light of magic into our mundane existence. Mary Ann is incredibly astute, and her conversations are a solace to my soul. Her beauty is a constant marvel that stirs within me a profound and ceaseless wonder. I had hoped but never dared to believe that I could find a woman to match Elizabeth's intelligence and grace. And yet, now Mary Ann is beside me, and my prayers have been answered.

My dear daughter Sarah, now blossoming into her fourteenth year, finds in Mary Ann not just the guidance of a housekeeper but the kinship of a sister. Their bond is a source of untold joy, a reminder of the unlikely harmony that can emerge from life's unforeseen pathways.

Yet, even as my heart swells with gratitude for the sanctuary we have found on Norfolk Island, the space and silence are expanding with the continued removal of its people. The departure of fifty-one souls aboard the Lady Nelson and the preparations to send another sixty-two on the Estramina render our community ever more sparse. In this quietude, though, there is little peace for I am faced now with the challenge of maintaining the spirits of those who remain. I have placed an increased investment into the island's entertainment, gathering the community together to share stories, song and dance to strengthen the bonds that remain and rouse them for the adventure ahead.

And still, the question of the future destination for my family hangs before me, a riddle yet to be solved. I still do not know whether to join our brethren in Van Diemen's Land or to seek out new horizons. While many options swirl around, I stand firm in my resolve to chart a course not beholden to Macarthur's machinations, to build a wealth untainted by the division that he sows.

In my nightly prayers, I lay my fears and hopes before the Lord, seeking His guidance and mercy. May He watch over Mary Ann and our unborn child, grant them health and happiness, and afford me the wisdom to lead and provide for my family amidst these uncertainties. With a heart laden with concern yet buoyed by faith, I pray for strength to be a protector and provider and to steer my family safely through these trying times.

23 August 1808

There is a sombre stillness that has enshrouded our home, the aftermath of a maelstrom of such searing intensity that I find myself grappling for reprieve. It was merely a few days ago that we were blessed with the birth of twin sons—a double joy that promised to burgeon into a lifetime of pride and happiness. They were named Hugh and John, two symbols of hope, cradled in the loving arms of their mother, Mary Ann, whose heart swelled with the pride of motherhood and the fulfillment of birthing boys.

Yet, as quickly as joy announced its arrival, it was chased away by the cruel hand of sorrow. Today, we faced the harrowing and unbearable loss of Hugh. He was so very fragile, and his passing has created a pain never before known to me. The gut-wrenching grief that grips Mary Ann is a mirror to my own—two parents united in anguish that words fail to convey. A son, particularly in these times, is more than just a child; he is the bearer of a family's name, a continuance of lineage, and a vessel for hopes and aspirations that stretch beyond the mere bounds of individual lifetimes.

In the wake of Hugh's passing, we are left to navigate a world that seems dimmer; the weight of our loss falls across every joy we might have known. The customs of our time dictate a sombre farewell to such an innocent soul; his earthly vessel, tender and untouched by the world's toil, was laid to rest amidst the wildflowers. A simple, quiet ceremony and a small cross to mark his presence among us, however fleeting.

I now turn to Sarah, my darling daughter, for strength. Her care for Mary Ann is a duty she conducts with a tenderness well beyond her age. Together, we weather the storm of our shared sorrow, finding in each other the support needed to endure the unendurable.

Amidst this personal heartache, the island continues to unravel, with Estramina's departure on the fifteenth of May further diminishing our numbers. The fabric of our small community grows ever thinner, the sense of isolation deepening with each farewell. As I see each adult and child onto the ship and bid each of my people farewell, I am reminded of the ceaseless tides of change that spare none.

In my prayers, I find myself searching for answers, my voice a whisper amid the roaring silence of loss. I ask the Lord what I may have done to be so tested, to have my heart so wrung. I beseech Him to envelop Hugh in His boundless mercy, to keep my son cradled in His tender care. In this hour of despair, I am a shattered father, striving to be a pillar of faith for a woman cloaked in mourning. May the Lord grant us the strength to bear this burden and find the fortitude to continue for the sake of John.

14 October 1809

In the waning light of an October day, as the world outside prepares for the quiet slumber of the evening, our home has been ripped apart. I have had to make a revelation that has torn the fabric of trust to its very core. It fell upon me, with hands that trembled and a heart heavy with shame, to confess to her my gravest sin—a betrayal that soon will manifest in the birth of another child. It is a child borne of my weakness and which I conceived with Elizabeth Nichols, a girl no older than my daughter Sarah. Mary Ann, whose heart has been a well of sorrow since the loss of our dear Hugh, has been dealt another, most grievous blow.

The telling of this truth was a deed more harrowing than any I have faced, and the wrath that it unleased in Mary Ann was so forceful that it shook the very foundation of my being. Her face, already tainted with sorry, became covered with the rawest of human agonies. The red that rose in her cheeks was not the flush of warmth I had known but the crimson tide of a rage born of betrayal. Her words, once tender and soothing, now lashed out with a venom that left no doubt as to the depth of her fury. With a voice rising to a pitch that seemed to claw at the heavens, she accused me of being the harbinger of our son's death, declaring that my sin had woven the shroud that now lay upon Hugh.

The air itself felt charged with the poison of my transgression, and as she spoke, the spit of her words seemed to etch themselves into the walls and into my soul. Never could I have envisioned such a storm brewing within the heart of my caring Mary Ann; never could I have fathomed the wildness my actions would drive her to.

The weight of her condemnation, the spectre of her fury, has left me reeling, questioning the very essence of my existence. The fear that her words may carry a harrowing truth—that my indiscretions may indeed have caused the suffering of our son—is a possibility that is inflicting profound pain. The thought that I may never again find grace in her eyes, nor in my own reflection, is a sentence I can scarcely bear.

In desperation, I turned to Sarah, my daughter, whose strength and composure have become the lifeline to which we both now cling. It is she who has become my comforter and she who attempts to soothe Mary Ann's soul.

Now, as I sit alone, in the silence of an abode fractured by my own doing, I turn my gaze to the Almighty, seeking support that seems, at this time, as distant as the stars. I beg Him to envelop Hugh in the sanctuary of His love and cradle the innocent soul that knew only a fleeting dawn. And for Mary Ann, I beseech Him to temper her anguish with the balm of His mercy, to guide her through this crucible to a place where forgiveness may yet bloom amidst the thorns of sorrow.

For myself, I am resigned to accept whatever penance He deems just, to carry the burden of my sin with a contrite heart and a soul aching for redemption. It is in His hands that

I lay my fate, humbled and broken, as I seek the path to atonement through my human frailty. I am faulty dear Lord, sinful, and I seek your forgiveness. Please show me the way to heal the wounds I have wrought.

TO THE HEART OF THE MAN

4 March 1810

As I pen this entry, the fabric of our lives is being delicately rewoven, tinged with the recent weeks' joy and sorrow. Amongst the threads of light, of great love, there are also lines of a dark legacy, strings that have caused so much suffering. Elizabeth's delivery of a son, Norfolk, has draped our family in layers of complex emotions. While Elizabeth's heart swells with the joy of motherhood, mine is entangled in my obligations towards Mary Ann, whose world I have irrevocably altered. Elizabeth is due to depart soon with her father for Van Diemen's Land. Her father will not shake my hand, choosing to shun the one who has cast his daughter into shame. I do not blame him, for I contemplate how I would respond if my own daughter, Sarah, were to be used for pleasurable advantage and then abandoned, especially by one who was meant to serve and protect the people. I harbour no ill will towards her father and, to make some amends, have ensured that she goes to Van Diemen's land laden with a sizeable dowry that will support her entire family.

On the ledger, I stated that she owns assets encompassing two hundred sheep, four cattle, fifteen swine, forty goats, fifteen acres under cultivation and a robust two-story dwelling. This will put her and our son in good stead for their new life in Van Diemen's Land, where these will, over time, be repaid to her. I hope that for her and her father, this shows my deep-seated desire to ensure her and Norfolk's wellbeing. Such assets will also make her an attractive wife, and I am enquiring about suitable husbands in her new home. It grieves me to know that I will not be in Van Diemen's Land to see my son Norfolk grow. And yet, I am blessed with John and will do all I can to protect him and see him grow into a gentleman.

As if my family's current traumatic circumstances were insufficient to test our mettle and faith, I received an edict from Governor Macquarie. It beckons me back to Port Jackson and advises of the return of our regiment to England. This unexpected mandate has taken me by great surprise, unsettling my very foundation. I suspect that this decision is rooted in a quest for administrative unity and, perhaps, a strategic bolstering against France. It may assist in securing the colony and England, but it delivers grave uncertainty for our future lives.

The notion of returning to England after a decade stirs a vast range of emotions. I am excited with the prospect of seeing my family again, but unsure of how they will react to my domestic situation. My children will know their cousins and aunts, which warms my heart. I long for my homeland but will miss the chance I have to input into the colony's creation. I am pleased with the thought that Mary Ann and Sarah will come to know England, and yet the imminent departure from Norfolk Island evokes a significant sense of loss. This island, with its majestic cliffs, verdant meadows, and ancient woodlands, has been a silent witness to the ebb and flow of our lives. Its natural splendour will be a cherished memory. And yet, perhaps it is timely to move onto a new place, to create new memories together as a family and to use this uncertainty to unite us.

In the face of this transition, my heart is particularly burdened with the grief that envelops Mary Ann. The joy of embarking on a new journey is marred by the sorrow of her recent loss and the lingering dark legacy of my past betrayal. I dearly hope that the bustling life of Port Jackson, with its array of entertainments and lively markets — will offer her a distraction from her despair. I, too, am eager to partake in the dances full of action and vigour that I have sorely missed here on the island. I know Elizabeth will become a great friend to Mary Ann, and I look forward to Sarah having the chance to be guided by her eldest daughter in the ways of women.

For this reason, I have asked Macquarie to grant me a stay of several months in Port Jackson to organise my affairs. I have also told, not asked, that I will be accompanied by Mary Ann, Sarah and John on the journey to England and asked that fitting arrangements be made for their utmost comfort. I hope that this knowledge provides a sense of security for Mary Ann, allowing her to feel safe in our union once again.

As we prepare to bid farewell to the serene beauty of Norfolk Island, my prayers are with those who remain. I pray for those last trusted residents left on the island and the safe transit of all. I shall miss this island desperately, and yet its memory will now always be tainted with death.

TO THE HEART OF THE MAN

10 September 1811

As the dawn crests, painting the sky with strokes of gold, Port Jackson is bustling, alive with activity. The air is crisp and yet comes with the promise of a warm spring. Our vessel, the Providence, stands majestic at the quay. Her sails have not yet been freed to meet the breeze, but still she stands, a striking example of human endeavour and the spirit of exploration. Her hull, sturdy and strong, is laden with the remnants of the 102nd Regiment, my beloved family, and a cargo most unique — four black swans, a gift from Macquarie to his friend Mr Birnie, and a kangaroo destined, I hope, for my delivery to the Prince of Wales.

The Providence is a vessel of considerable repute, and her crew is well-seasoned by the whims of the sea. The camaraderie among the men brings me great confidence, their faces etched with the tales of voyages past and the anticipation of the journey ahead. Beyond the living treasures bound for distant shores, our cargo is a collection of the colony's finest exports, goods that speak of the land's bounty and the industriousness of its people. It is a remarkably different atmosphere to that of the ships laden with convicts, smelling of faeces and fear that brought me to this place. I go back now with an air of triumph and excitement to show what has been created thus far.

John, at the tender age of three, is standing more like a boy and far less like a baby; his days are filled with the boundless energy and curiosity of his age. His laughter is a constant melody, and I am sure it will bring us much-needed joy during our voyage. I am worried about how he, being so young, will endure the sea sickness and wild weather we are bound to encounter. I have no doubt, though, that wrapped in the arms of his loving mother, father and sister, he will find his footing. Sarah and Mary Ann, having basked in the genteel society of Port Jackson, carry with them the elegance and refinement learned in the company of Elizabeth and her daughters. Their time was spent in a flurry of social engagements, cultural exchanges, and the cultivation of friendships that have enriched their souls and broadened their horizons.

They did not, however, enjoy the regular teasing from the boys who brought them all sorts of spiders and snakes, never seen on Norfolk Island. We were fortunate to be here in the cooler months when such beasts retreat from the bitter winds and frosts. Otherwise, the lads would have been tempted to show these girls a greater selection of frightful creatures. I am glad also that there is less chance for John, with his curious wanderings, to be unwittingly injured by this land's wildlife. Unfortunately, despite the attempt of many Irishmen to grace their land with soil from their motherland, we have found nothing that prevents snakes from crossing into our communities. I have heard many a convict and settler surmise that this is a sign that they have surely landed in hell.

Over the past few months, I have also been relieved to witness Mary Ann's countenance return to that which I first admired on Norfolk Island. Her heart appears to have shed the shroud of bitterness and grief and opened again to the wonders and opportunities around her. I am sure that I have Elizabeth to thank for this, as she has been a constant companion and counsel to Mary Ann. My darling Mary Ann could have no better guide as to how to traverse the chaos of the colony and her new home in England. I suspect too, Elizabeth is teaching her well about the ways of men and arming her with both personal responsibility and cutting retorts. She would have used this chance to share with Mary Ann what is fantasy and what is reality, and prepared her well for the latter. For what is Elizabeth if not a friend who is intent to keep me honest and my womenfolk healthy.

While I know it pains Elizabeth to be once again without her husband, I must admit to a great feeling of relief. Macarthur has been sent to England by the new Governor (and yet a known force) Foveaux to defend his actions after the rebellion. Ever the opportunist, Macarthur is using the occasion to develop trade along the route, now dabbling in spices and sandalwood. Elizabeth has confided in me her concerns that her husband will be at the mercy of an unsupportive and even hostile administration in England and fears for what may eventuate after his trial. I have listened to her also tell of their increasingly tenuous financial position. Much of the trade Macarthur was relying upon has fallen through to the point that they may need to sell his properties in Port Jackson. Even for a man so brutal, this loss would come as a painful blow.

I feel for Elizabeth and her family in this time of uncertainty and wish that I could provide more than a friendly ear. This situation cements for me the ever-changing nature of our fortunes. I did never think I would see the day when Macarthur would crumble; it is a dire warning for us all about the fickle nature of fate and a lesson I hope that I never have to learn directly.

My dear Sarah has bloomed under the tutelage of her peers, now leaving Port Jackson almost unrecognisable from the girl who entered. She is undoubtedly a beautiful, generous and gentile woman who will make a favourable wife. I hope to find her a suitable match on our return to England and set her up there for a life of comfort. I often look at this dear girl and wonder how I came to be blessed with such a pure spirit. She never ceases to bring me pride.

The prospect of sailing to England via China is simply exciting. Tales of Asia's exotic lands, of cultures so vastly different from our own, have long filled my imagination. The mystique of China, with its ancient customs, splendid architecture, and rich history, offers us the opportunity for a true adventure. I am so proud to share this experience with my family and steward them through this strange new world. Yet, I am also plagued by a gnawing worry. It is knowing what may unfold upon this vessel. I have seen what horrors may await us. I still have nightmares about the harrowing journeys aboard the Pitt and Hillsborough.

There are some nights when the anguish still awakens me. The visions of what I witnessed aboard these sadistic ships seem so real; the bodies covered in sores, scorched by the sun, plastered by the salt, wrapped in sails and thrust into the sea. The spectre of the past casts a large shadow, and so I board with grave concern for the welfare of my family amidst both the unpredictable ways of the ocean and the all too frequent storms of man.

Our companions, the black swans and the kangaroo, symbols of this land's unique and wondrous fauna, are entrusted to my care. While many of the crew joke that I am Captain of the creatures, the truth is that their wellbeing is paramount, a responsibility I bear with honour, for they are not merely animals but ambassadors. It is my fervent hope that they, alongside us, will weather the voyage with resilience, reaching the shores of England as evidence of the marvels of our distant colony.

Tonight, as the stars emerge to keep vigil over the night, my thoughts turn to prayer. I beseech the Almighty for His guidance and protection, for a swift and safe passage across the vast expanse that lies before us. May the winds be ever in our favour, the seas calm and forgiving, and the Providence steadfast in her course. For my family, comrades, and our precious cargo, I pray for a journey marked not by the trials of the past but by the promise of new beginnings.

TO THE HEART OF THE MAN

24 March 2012

I have now settled my family in our lodgings in London, and we have finally found our land legs again. The journey from Port Jackson, while difficult for my family, was far more than just a tedious and trying transit. It has been an odyssey filled with new sights and sounds, which our family has shared. The Providence bore us away from the familiar shores and deposited us into realms that defied our imaginations.

The early days of our journey were a battle not with the sea itself but with the malaise it wrought upon our bodies. Sea sickness was a relentless foe, laying us low with its invisible hand. It took several days to get over the worst of the symptoms, and yet for Mary Ann, the nausea seemed to remain right throughout the voyage. Our accommodations aboard the Providence were modest and compact, and within these shared quarters, Mary Ann, Sarah, John, and I found harmony. The constraints of our cabin, which was almost cave-like, fostered a closeness, a unity amongst our clan that created great comfort amidst the endless expanse of the ocean.

Our meals, often a simple fare of salted meat, hardtack, and the occasional blessing of fresh catch or preserved fruits, were initially a source of displeasure, a sign that in many ways we had become soft. As hunger set in though, preferences for finer food became irrelevant and those rations we once sneered at became the sustenance we looked forward to.

Upon our arrival in China, the shock was immediate and profound. The sheer number of people was overwhelming, as were the architectural marvels we beheld. This land was a stark contrast to the sprawling natural landscapes, the space and the modest settlements of Port Jackson and Norfolk Island. Mary Ann and Sarah, with their innate curiosity and wonder, were immediately captivated by the towering pagodas and imperial palaces, their intricate designs and vibrant colours. Our guides and interpreters told of a society steeped in millennia of history and tradition, of emperors and wars, and of the philosophies of life that bind them.

The teeming streets, alive with a vast diversity of people, were a spectacle that none of us had ever witnessed nor would ever have been brave enough to imagine. The bustling marketplaces, overflowing with exotic goods and the hum of commerce, offered a sensory overload. Sarah, in particular, was drawn to the array of silks and porcelains, her eyes wide with the realisation of the world's vast richness. Mary Ann, ever the observer, took a keen interest in the social customs and etiquette, the interactions that wove the fabric of Chinese society. Our time in China, while short, will be a memory that will stay in our hearts and minds for many years to come. While the souvenirs may break and shred seeing this unique culture, and sharing it as a family are gifts that will never give up their magnificence.

The arrival in Portsmouth was a return to a familiar place for me, yet a strange new one for my family. When I stepped foot on the shores, I knew I was no longer the same man that had left her several years earlier. I disembarked a Captain and former Lieutenant Governor of Norfolk Island. I had a family in tow, one I now must seek to build a good life for here in England. I have worked hard in the colonies to show my capabilities, and now it is time to seek a station that befits my skills and dedication.

Settling into our lodgings in London, we struggled to acclimate to the rhythms of a city vastly different from the colonies. The colder climes of March, so different from the warmth of Norfolk Island, were an uncomfortable reminder of our new reality. Yet, within this bustling metropolis, Mary Ann and Sarah found their stride, their spirits invigorated by the endless possibilities that lay before them. By the fire at night, watching them discuss the latest fashions and follies of the city is a great source of joy. Beside the hearth, as I play with John and listen to their plans for the following day, I realise that we can make any place home.

The announcement of Mary Ann's pregnancy was a happy occasion and had us realising that the sickness on the journey was not caused by the endless movement of the sea but by the life stirring within her. The child is due in Autumn and will be a dearly sought-after addition to our family. John continues to grow stronger and more capable each day and will be four when the new child arrives. However, amidst this cause for celebration, there was also disappointment. I received news that the kangaroo, our gift intended for the Prince of Wales, had been claimed by the Royal Society. Banks keeps a firm grip over the flora and fauna that enter England from the colonies and is intent on inspecting and cataloguing every new entry before allowing it on to its final destination. I cannot help but think perhaps Banks has kept this kangaroo to deliver to the prince himself, hindering my chance to escalate my reputation and position. Mary Ann counsels me not to take it personally, that it is only politics, and yet it appears this is a game that I need to get better at playing.

Lord, thank you for landing us safe here in England. My heart is filled with gratitude for the experiences that you have granted us. I pray for a flourishing future for our family here and for the peace and prosperity of those we left behind.

12 July 1812

Recent events have made it clear to me that reinvention of oneself is a necessity. I have finally received my assignment. I am to join the 100th Regiment at Winchester. While I can see how this position would be a stepping stone, it also feels like a slap in the face. I have spent seventeen years providing unwavering service in the colonies. Seventeen years of toiling and dedicating every ounce of my energy for purposeful ends. Still, there is no recognition for the responsibilities I bore or the success that I delivered. This is a naught but pitiful acknowledgement for all that I have done in the name of those in power. They choose, instead of congratulating me, to cast me aside. Is this because of my time with Macarthur? Is this a blight on my reputation that is still bringing me down? If so, I must work harder to shift out of this shadow.

At thirty-nine, the urgency to elevate my position within the military hierarchy is not merely a professional pursuit but a personal imperative. The impending arrival of another child only serves to amplify this pressure. A growing family means that I must force myself forward if I am to secure their comfort and my legacy. This is a pivotal moment that demands a strategic realignment of my affiliations and a deliberate distancing from the influence of Macarthur. In many ways, I must start again and build a profile that will be attractive to those men pulling the strings.

Governor Macquarie's endorsement, glowing though it may be, has made me realise that advancement is not solely the product of one's achievements but also of perception. Mary Ann, ever my pillar of strength and now with Elizabeth's wisdom, clearly sees the path that lies before me. Her belief in my potential is unwavering, her counsel sagacious. She understands I do not share the same shrewdness or flair for political manoeuvring as many of my peers. And so, she urges me to elevate not only my aspirations but my appearance, to embody the very essence of the position I seek to attain.

Heeding her advice, I ventured into the tailor's, a domain where fabric and thread intertwine to craft not just garments but guises, not just suits, but selfhoods. The air was thick with the scent of fresh textiles, the hum of conversation punctuated by the snip of scissors and the rolling of tape. It was a world unto itself, a place where social standing could be woven from the loom of ambition.

With Mary Ann's superior sense of style to guide me, I selected pieces that spoke not just of fashion but of authority. I chose waistcoats of fine wool, pantaloons that hugged the form with a commanding elegance, a crimson silk sash that whispered distinction, and a breastplate that gleamed with the promise of pride. The breeches were tailored to perfection, and to complete the ensemble, pearl buttons, each one a symbol of my integrity and attention to detail.

As I stepped out of the tailor's, I could not help but feel transformed. While much of my new attire would still take several weeks to stitch, it had already seemed to weave itself into the very fabric of my resolve. Yet, beneath the surface of the confidence brought by the clothes lies a torrent of frustration — a bitterness born of years of dedication seemingly overlooked, of potential yet to be fully recognised. Still, I have shone through before and will do so again.

Mary Ann's faith in me bolsters my spirit, propelling me forward in pursuit of a better station. The workload is immense, and there are many meetings to be had with men who may elevate my position, but I am firm in my resolve. The pressure to succeed, to secure a future worthy of my family's sacrifices, is a task that I take on willingly.

Tonight, as I pen these reflections, I offer a prayer for my parents. I am only now realising the responsibility they bore, and the work and the worry that went on behind the scenes of the Inn, the burdens they bore to bring about a good life and an enduring legacy. May my efforts bring achievements that will make my father, mother and Mary Ann proud.

TO THE HEART OF THE MAN

29 September 1812

With a sorrow too tortuous for words, we have laid to rest our dear James, whose fragile life left him after a mere nine days. We are engulfed in a grief that is wide and deep and which defies consolation. The doctor confessed his uncertainty regarding the cause of our loss, suggesting only that the rigours of our recent journey might have compromised the child's development. While Mary Ann has not spoken of this suggestion further, it remains a palpable presence between us and has sown seeds of guilt within my heart.

I cannot bear the thought that my family is suffering yet again because of me. If only I had worked harder to secure a better position for us in Port Jackson, we would never have had to undertake the journey. If I had the nous to find favour with the power brokers there and suppressed some of my principles, I could now well be a profitable landowner, and we would never have had to make the voyage that may have taken James from us. If I had the courage to leave the Corps, as Elizabeth suggested, we would not now be in this situation. In the weight of grief, I also make a vow to myself to make up for this loss and provide for my family a life that will provide all the brightness possible to cast out this sorrow.

The funeral for James was a quiet affair, a small gathering under the grey expanse of the London sky. Our close congregation of family and friends stood by a grave too tiny, the air filled with the muted sounds of sobs and clouded by our collective heartache. The simple wooden coffin was adorned with a single bouquet of wildflowers, picked by Sarah's own hands, her only way of working through this tragedy. Mary Ann is much changed, spending her days in silent tears, unable to speak of the pain she feels. Does she blame me? I believe the way she pulls away suggests scorn and shame. This treatment, while it hurts like barbs in my heart, only strengthens my resolve to give her only the very best that this life can offer. I will deliver her from this sorrow, somehow.

Despite my reticence, I decided to accept Macarthur's invitation for a meeting. At this time, I must look at all options before me to make a better life for my family, and I must do what I can by providing any counsel that may assist Elizabeth. Macarthur laid bare the treacherous landscape of his own circumstances. The commercial world is now full of hazards, making his mercantile endeavours, once profitable, now perilous. The situation is so bad that it threatens to engulf his family and drive them into destitution. He was once so sure of success; now, his projects have been revealed as mere gambles and have trapped him in a web of debt and doubt. Part of me wanted to feel pride, for finally, it appeared I was in a more fruitful position. It would have been easy to chide him and assert that these are fair consequences for his past corruption.

But I am called to be a man of integrity, and I will not do what he did to Patterson - spit on a man when he is down.

Elizabeth was right to be concerned about how her husband would be regarded in England. He has been tainted here as the instigator of the rebellion and ordered to be arrested and tried if he ever sets foot in the colony again. So, Macarthur is in a bind that is breaking his heart. Either he remains in the relative safety of England and leaves the dismantling of his legacy to his family, or he returns to Port Jackson at great personal risk, possibly to face the punishments that he rightly deserves. Of course, I know which pathway I would take, but Macarthur's selfishness still clouds his ability to see any clear way forward.

And yet, beneath Macarthur's personal priorities, he did find time to share his belief in my potential. He counselled me in the ways to find a station befitting my aspirations, and urged me to use my convivial character to forge meaningful connections. Perhaps I was wrong about him, or maybe his current dilemma has changed his perspectives, but he does seem to want the best for my future. This support is greatly appreciated, although it also adds to my stress. I cannot admit to him that the pressure Mary Ann is placing on me to ascend is, in the face of our recent sorrow, almost unsustainable. It seems that striving is a sign of strength, and if so, then I need to become much tougher.

Now, in these quiet hours of reflection, when both Mary Ann and Sarah have rejected my company in favour of their grief, and John is slumbering soundly, I allow myself to cry and call out to the Lord. Please, God, embrace our beloved James and place him beside his brother Hugh, holding them gently in your eternal love. I beseech You, cease punishing my dear Mary Ann for my weaknesses. If it pleases You, Lord, continue Your retribution against me. I will take all the lessons you have to give with dignity. But please spare my innocent family from further suffering.

17 May 1813

In a turn of events that feels nothing short of miraculous, my relentless pursuit of forging constructive contacts has borne fruit in a manner most extraordinary. Today, I was graced with an offer from Lord Bathurst himself, a figure of considerable influence and authority, who currently holds the position of Secretary of State for War and the Colonies. His Lordship has decided to appoint me as the Naval Officer to the Port of Port Jackson. This is an absolute and profound honour.

The role of Naval Officer is a position of significant responsibility and prestige. I am to be entrusted with the oversight of maritime activities, customs, and duties in the port — a vital cog in the colony's economic and security apparatus. It is a role that demands a keen understanding of naval affairs, an unimpeachable morality, and a commitment to the crown's interests. This role places me at the very centre of the commercial world of the colony and makes me a man of great influence. I can see already how I will need to precariously juggle the interests of a multitude of stakeholders, and I pray to the Lord to give me strength to serve with impeccable integrity.

The salary attached to this position, a substantial four hundred pounds a year, is a sum that dwarfs the earnings of a normal officer and represents a seismic shift in my family's fortunes. This income, substantial by any measure, heralds a new era of financial security and comfort for us. To signify our change in station, Mary Ann has taken on the name Henrietta Maria, to be used now at all formal events. With this new title she is securing her status well away from her convict forefathers and positioning herself so wisely in the eyes of the women here. It also pays a fitting tribute to our dearest friend, Elizabeth Macarthur, who shares this aristocratic appellation.

Our departure is set for the twenty-sixth day of August aboard the vessel General Hewitt. Mary Ann is once again with child, and the worry for her wellbeing and that of our unborn baby is a constant companion to my thoughts. The knowledge that we will be travelling with three hundred convicts adds a layer of concern and has created many sleepless nights. The suffering of these souls, the first-hand witness to their plight, is a harrowing prospect. I have seen it all before, but I cannot stand for Mary Ann and my children to be privy to such torment. Additionally, with increased numbers, especially convicts, the risks of disease are compounded. My resolve to shield my family from these perils is unwavering. Please, Lord, keep us under your protection.

In preparation for our arrival, there is much to be done — securing land and lodging to serve as the foundation of our new life in Port Jackson. Yet, it is the prospect of establishing my stables that fills me with ardent fervour, akin to that of a young man embarking on his first adventure. The substantial salary affords me the luxury of importing thoroughbred horses, a long-held dream that is now tantalizingly within reach.

As I contemplate the future, I am buoyed by a sense of optimism that this appointment is indeed the commencement of my rise. Mary Ann shares this sentiment and is already in consultation with the ladies in her inner circle to make preparations to purchase the clothing and household ornaments that will befit her new role and present our family accordingly. The recognition of my efforts, the just reward for years of toil, feels like a vindication of my belief in the virtue of hard work. Lord Bathurst's faith in me lights the path forward, guiding me towards a destiny that I have long envisioned but as yet dared not claim as my own. Now is my time to take it.

Tonight, as I retire to my study, my heart is full of gratitude for the opportunities that are unfolding. I pray for the health and safety of my beloved Mary Ann and our unborn child, for my dear daughter Sarah and little John. Then there are also prayers for the children I have left behind, John, Mary Ann and Norfolk. Please, Lord, watch over them and lead them to a full and fruitful life. Provide me with the strength to navigate the challenges ahead and to steward the responsibilities of my new role with wisdom. This is the dawn of our ascent, the foundation upon which our future prosperity will be built. It now rests upon me to ensure this foundation stays firm.

TO THE HEART OF THE MAN

6 February 1814

As dawn breaks over the horizon, heralding our imminent arrival in Port Jackson, it is with great relief that we spy the shores of New South Wales. The journey aboard the General Hewitt has been nothing short of gruelling, a test of endurance that has left its mark on us all. The ship, while sturdy, became a crucible of suffering for its human cargo, with thirty-two souls succumbing to the dire conditions on board. The stifling heat, compounded by relentless storms and rain, forced us to seek refuge below deck, a decision that weighed heavily on young John, rendering him disruptive and grumpy, a disturbing contrast to his usual spirited self. His irritability impacted upon us all, straining our relationships and testing our ability to remain considerate and polite.

Amidst the myriad experiences that have imprinted upon us during our voyage aboard the General Hewitt, none have been more harrowing than the plight of the convicts who shared our passage. The conditions they endured were a stark reminder of the inhumanity that can pervade the souls of men when driven by indifference. Confined below deck in cramped, squalid quarters, they were subjected to an existence that barely afforded them the dignity of being human. Disease ran rampant, a silent thief stealing away the vitality of those already stripped of their freedom. Each day brought with it the grim ritual of witnessing bodies, shrouded only in shredded sails, being consigned to the depths of the ocean, a final, ignoble end to lives marked by injustice.

For Sarah and Mary Ann, the spectacle of death and despair that unfolded before their eyes created much sorrow, etching into their hearts a memory that will forever colour their perception of the world. The sight of fellow beings, however flawed or fallen in the eyes of the law, being treated with such callous disregard for their intrinsic worth as human beings was a profound shock. To see life extinguished and disposed of with such ease left them with a deep-seated awareness of the fragility of existence, a realization that the line between life and oblivion is perilously thin.

This experience, while agonizing, has imbued both Sarah and Mary Ann with a heightened regard for the sanctity of human life. It has instilled in them a resolve to never overlook the suffering of others and to always remember the faces and fates of those who perished in silence on that ship. The memory of the General Hewitt and its cargo of despair will remain with them as both a reminder of the depths of endurance the human spirit is capable of and the preciousness of the life they are fortunate enough to continue. Though heavy with the weight of what they have witnessed, their hearts now understand the compassion needed in this world.

Amidst the tumult of our voyage, life found a way to assert its supremacy with the birth of Hugh Hewitt on board. His arrival, under the most challenging of circumstances, stands as a tribute not only to my brother and his namesake but to the resilience of our family. Our journey has also been marked by an unexpected blossoming of love. Sarah found her heart entwined with that of Alfred Thrupp, a crewman whose presence on the General Hewitt has forever altered the course of our lives. While there was so much heartache upon the voyage, watching this pair fall in love, share lingering looks and whisper together well into the night was simply wonderful. Their swift engagement is evidence of the unpredictable nature of love, kindling a flame of joy that will soon be celebrated in matrimony. As we disembark, I do so not only as a father but as a soon-to-be father-in-law, eagerly anticipating the union of two kindred spirits.

In Port Jackson, we have secured lodgings near the port to facilitate my duties as the newly appointed Naval Officer. In addition, I have acquired "The Retreat" at Vaucluse, leased from Sir Maurice O'Connell, to provide a sanctuary away from the docks. This holiday home offers a haven of peace with its sweeping views and tranquil surroundings, a place where our family can rejuvenate and regain perspective away from the raucousness and politics of the port.

I am almost beside myself with anticipation for the arrival of Wellington, the first English thoroughbred with a fully authorized pedigree to grace our shores. Wellington will be but the beginning of my legacy of equine excellence. He will join my expanding stable and help me build an illustrious horse racing tradition in this new nation. There are many blessings that come from the responsibility that Lord Bathurst has afforded me, but none so precious as to surround myself with such majestic creatures.

Tonight, as we settle into our new lodgings, I pray for the souls lost on our journey, for the health and happiness of our growing family, and for the prosperity of all who seek a new beginning in the colony. May our time here be met with success and may the legacy I build suitably honour the God that has guided us across many seas, through many storms, and back to Port Jackson.

11 February 1816

As the sun sets on this day, I find myself in a state of reflection, marvelling at the journey that has led me to this point. Yesterday, I was joined in matrimony with my beloved Mary Ann. Many mused, even jested that this ceremony was merely a consequence of Governor Macquarie's new edict, which compels all women within the colony to present a marriage certificate to receive government stores. While this might have been the catalyst for our union in the eyes of the law, for me, it was merely an affirmation of a commitment that existed deep within my heart. My vows were not mere words but a solemn promise to elevate Mary Ann to a position of respect and admiration, befitting her grace and strength through years of adversity.

The wedding was as grand an affair that could be arranged at short notice. It was a celebration befitting my stature and was set against the backdrop of a colony that is rapidly evolving under Macquarie's stewardship. We were joined by Elizabeth and her family and enjoyed a wedding dinner in Vaucluse House full of the very best food this colony has to offer. In her wise way, Mary Ann also ensured that we were joined by both the elite and the emancipists, showing that we held no favour to any faction, but were determined to do right by all peoples.

We shared the ceremony with our children, including the latest blessing, George. He was born last year, but I was too afraid to pen the pregnancy lest I push my favours with our Lord. I send Him thanks and praise for the cessation of Mary Ann's miscarriages and, thus, my punishment. The joy George's presence brings is immeasurable, and he is taken well care of by his mother and big brother, John, who is now eight and growing into a strapping and serious young man. Hugh is three and in continual mischief, making for weary days for the Nannies who attempt to restrain his curiosity.

The news of the birth of my first grandchild, Frances, fills me with joy, both at the safe birth of the child and at the continuation of our lineage. The anticipation of Sarah's return from Van Diemen's Land, is also cause for celebration, and I do finally feel that I am creating the right foundation for our future.

Now, as husband and wife, Mary Ann and I concentrate our efforts on the construction of Henrietta Villa. We have settled the purchase of the one hundred and ninety acres on Eliza Point and are ready to begin building our official residence. This is a bold endeavour but one that symbolizes not only our aspirations but also our commitment to creating an enduring legacy. I have engaged the convict architect Frances Greenway to design a magnificent mansion in the style of those I loved in Regent's Park in London. In the meantime, our residence here at Vaucluse House, with its modest farm and gorgeous gardens overlooking the ocean, provides a serene counterpoint to the bustling life of the colony. It is here, amid the soil rumoured to be blessed by Ireland itself, that we find peace and a sense of belonging in the years while Henrietta Villa takes shape.

I have secured several additional convicts as housekeepers to take care of the domestic duties so that Mary Ann can focus on the entertaining required of my role. There are many stakeholders to please, and so we find the best way is to enjoy their company and shower them with pleasantries. They are much more amiable to agree with my plans with a full stomach and buoyed by fine wine and spirits. This approach suits me much better than conniving conversations in dark hallways. I have found a way to use my friendliness, rather than force, to be a positive influence.

TO THE HEART OF THE MAN

22 September 1816

In the ebbs and flows of life, where joy and sorrow are interwoven, today stands as another reminder that there are blessings always to be found, even amongst the darkest nights. Today we welcomed another son into this world. He has been named Thomas, in honour of my dear brother. And just like his namesake, his presence brings with it a surge of indescribable joy.

Yet, the light that Thomas brings is tempered by a profound grief that lingers in the air like a silent fog. Merely two weeks ago, we laid to rest our beloved George, a child who, in his brief year with us, had become an irreplaceable part of our hearts. The anguish of his loss is a wound that time will struggle to heal, for he had woven himself so deeply into the fabric of our family that his absence leaves a void no words can fill.

As Mary Ann and I navigate this swirl of emotions, the arrival of Thomas is both a blessing and a reminder of the burdens that we bear as parents, how we must work hard to keep this son safe; lest he too be taken from our hands. How I wish to cling to them, all of my children. How I wish to close them in and cover them in cleanliness and comfort. However, I know that this extreme approach would be futile; the Lord has the final determination between life and death.

The funeral for George, held in the heart of Port Jackson, was a ceremony filled with solemn grace, a moment to honour a life too briefly lived. Gathered with close friends and family, we committed his small body to the earth under the canopy of a sky that seemed to weep with us. The rites were simple, a reflection of the times and a testament to the sheer number of souls requiring the priest's attention on this day.

My tears were shed for George, but also for James, all alone in the cemetery back in London. The distance that separates us from his resting place is a chasm filled with longing and a stark reminder of the losses we leave along the pathways of our lives. My mind also turns to my other children, whom I may never know. My son John, born of Elizabeth is now ten, as is Mary Ann, born from Sarah. Norfolk would now be seven, and his mother, Elizabeth, I am sure, would be flourishing as a farmer on Van Diemen's land. Sometimes, I wish they would set out to find me, the man who is their father, so that I can see how they have grown under their mother's guidance. Although I am sure with every part of my being that Mary Ann would die from distress in their presence. These children are a threat to her very core.

As I hold Thomas in my arms, feeling the weight of his small form against my chest, I am reminded of the delicate balance of life, of the joy that can emerge from the depths of despair. I pray for the strength to guide him through this world, to show him the boundless love that Mary Ann and I have to give, even as our hearts grapple with the chaos of our recent loss. I had thought, perhaps naively, that we had found favour in the Lord's eyes and that the trials we faced were behind us. Yet, the duality of our current circumstance — a new life cradled in the arms of grief — suggests that my journey back to His flock is far from over.

Captain John Piper

2 November 1816

On this day, under the warm embrace of the spring sun, a day that shall forever be etched into the annals of my life, I, John Piper, have laid the foundation stone of Henrietta Villa. Amidst the fanfare and celebration, and with a heart swollen with pride, I watched my long-held dreams manifest into reality upon the hallowed grounds of Elizabeth Point.

The ceremony was a grand spectacle orchestrated by the esteemed society of military masons, whose honest companionship has provided unwavering support throughout my tenure and has greatly influenced my success. These brethren of the Masonic order have played an instrumental role in shaping our community, and today, were arrayed in all their regalia to celebrate the planting of this landmark.

The air resonated with the sounds of a fête champêtre as officers, gentlemen, and esteemed ladies, whom Mary Ann and I had the honour of hosting, journeyed by water to partake in this momentous occasion. Our procession, a riverine cortège that cut a ceremonial wake across the harbour, was a sight to behold. Upon disembarking, we proceeded in Masonic order, a solemn yet joyous parade that marked the commencement of this new chapter. We had the honour of serving one hundred Ladies and Gentlemen with a sumptuous dinner, after which there was so much merry dancing that my head was truly in a spin.

The foundation stone, now bearing the mark of this historic day, is not just the cornerstone of what will be a grand mansion but also a symbol of the path I have carved in this land. Inscribed upon it were the words that reflected the deep regard, admiration, and gratitude I hold for Governor Lachlan Macquarie, whose support has been as strong as the stone itself.

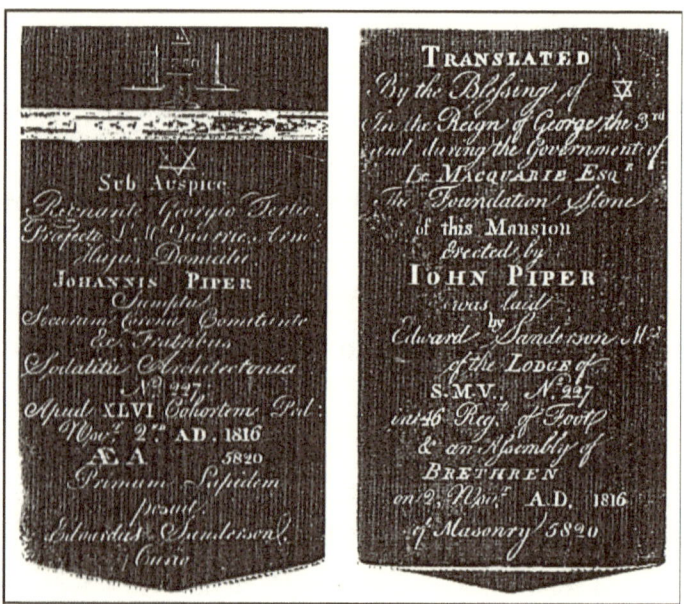

The foundation stone at Henrietta Villa

As the Masonic rites were observed and the foundation stone set, a symphony of trowels and hammers sang in harmony with the collective breath of the assembly. The air was filled with the fragrance of the freshly turned earth and the salt spray of the ocean.

Mary Ann, a shining example of elegance, stood by my side, her eyes reflecting the grandeur of the mansion that will rise from this foundation. The excitement that surged through us was a shared pulse, a rhythm that resonated with the very heartbeat of our family's future.

Later, as I stood amidst the gathering of esteemed guests, my gaze inevitably found its way to Mary Ann, whose appearance embodied sophistication. Clad in an exquisite gown that accentuated the regal contours of her posture, the rich fabric, silk of the deepest sapphire, flowed about her with a subtle whisper of opulence. Its Empire waistline drew the eye to her elegant form, and the fine lace detailing along the hem and neckline spoke of meticulous attention to decorum. A shawl of the softest cashmere rested upon her shoulders, a delicate embrace against the chill of the sea breeze. Her bonnet, trimmed with the tender bloom of spring flowers, framed her visage with a painterly perfection. In her presence, the air seemed to be still, the murmurs of the assembly hushed by the sheer force of her poise. She moved through the crowd with the ease of a gentle breeze, her every gesture further evidence of the refinement that she brought to our union.

As I observed her from across the lawn, I could not help but feel a surge of pride. To have Mary Ann as my wife was a blessing beyond measure. Her beauty was not merely in the garments she wore but in the strength, compassion, and intelligence that radiated from her very being. In her, I saw not just the mother of my children or the mistress of our soon-to-be-built Henrietta Villa but a partner whose spirit and heart were interwoven with my own.

Amidst the day's festivities, I began to imagine the halls of Henrietta Villa filled with laughter and life. I could already see the sweeping gardens taking shape, the thoroughbreds grazing in the paddocks and the sumptuous gatherings that would soon be a staple of our existence. I also imagined the racetrack I would build and the carnivals that would provide a great source of pleasure for the people of Port Jackson. And I praised the Lord for all of it, for what was already here and what is yet to come.

I retire this evening weary with the grand entertainments of the day but also with a heart brimming full of triumph. Under God's grace, we step forward into a future bright with possibility, and I offer a silent prayer for the flourishing of our family and the home that will be Henrietta Villa.

5 November 1819

This day finds me steeped in remorse so deep and dark it threatens to consume me whole. With a heavy heart and a burdened soul, I confess to having succumbed once more to the allures of sin. The social life that my status affords, replete with its incessant temptations, has proven too intense for my mortal resolve. Amid the whirlwind of our societal engagements, I have faltered grievously, ensnared by the beautiful affections of a girl named Sarah Hodgetts, who, at twenty-two, now carries the fruit of my indiscretion.

With her captivating charm and youthful grace, Sarah was a temptation I could not resist. Now she stands at the edge of motherhood, alone and undoubtedly frightened, and I am left to grapple with the consequences of my actions, which have destroyed the harmony of our home and Sarah's future.

The revelation of this transgression to my wife, my dear Mary Ann, was met with a fury that matched the force of the summer tempests. Her rage, righteous and raw, filled the air with a cacophony of pain and betrayal. She demanded, with a voice that brooked no argument, that I rid ourselves of this problem, that Sarah Hodgetts and the child she carries be cast away, sent to a place far from our sight. She refuses to have any of my bastard children near, a term which she spat at me in her anger. Her words scrape harshly against my already broken and bleeding conscience.

I understand Mary Ann's distress, as we have not long celebrated the first birthday of our first daughter together. She is named Elizabeth and is as radiant as her mother and my dear friend Elizabeth Macarthur combined. Mary Ann has found much joy in raising a daughter and shaping her into a strong young woman. But now I have stripped that peace away, punishing her with my dalliance and lack of discipline.

In the wake of her fury, I am left to navigate the wild waters of my own making. I have begun discreet and delicate inquiries into the possibility of establishing Sarah in Van Diemen's Land. The decision is fraught with complexity, each option a maze of moral considerations that weigh heavily upon me.

As I ponder the fate of Sarah Hodgetts and the innocent life she carries, I am reminded of just how fragile my reputation here is and the rapidity with which it can be fractured. The social standing I have fought so tirelessly to uphold now feels like a gilded cage, a trap of my own design. And yet the walls are weak, and so is my will.

In the stillness of the night, as I lay awake, tormented by the echoes of Mary Ann's wrathful words, I cannot help but question the path that has led me here. Is this the cost of my ambition? Is this the price of the life I have sought to build?

4 July 1820

Today, I find space and silence in a corner of my study, reflecting on news received with a blend of relief and hidden anguish. Sarah Hodgetts has given birth to a child in Van Diemen's Land, a daughter called Henrietta. It is a comfort to know that both mother and child are in good health, settled, and with sufficient resources to afford them a life of security and relative ease. However, it tears at my heart now every time I walk through these doors to know that the name given to my greatest achievement is also now born by a product of my sinfulness and shame. Nevertheless, the arrangements have been discreet, shielding them from the unforgiving societal gaze that too often falls upon such circumstances.

I have kept this news from Mary Ann, whose spirit has been consumed by the orchestration of our upcoming social engagements. To burden her with this knowledge would only fracture the fragile peace we've carefully constructed within our walls. It is a decision that weighs heavily upon me, for the silence I keep is a fortress of my own making, erected to protect her from further distress. Yet, the omission is a stone in my heart, a silent acknowledgment of the complexities of our lives now entwined with duty and appearance.

As Mary Ann delves into the intricacies of planning a three-day picnic and party, I watch her with a heart full of admiration and sorrow, knowing the delicate balance upon which our domestic harmony is perched. In my silent vigil, I can only pray that the decisions I have made will, in time, prove to heal the wounds of the past and not plant seeds of further pain.

20 April 1822

On this, the anniversary of my forty-ninth year, I find myself in quiet repose, reflecting upon the momentous occasion that this day has become. Not only does it mark another year of my life but also the day we officially take residence in Henrietta Villa. The symbolism is not lost on me; it is as though I am stepping across the threshold into a new era, solidifying my stance as a man who has carved his own path with resolve, respect and dedication to duty.

We make our entrance as a family expanded, with the joyful addition of Anne Christina Frances, a name fitting for the nobility that we have become. We now have three boys and two girls by our hearth. John, Hugh and Thomas are fourteen, nine and six and are showing themselves to be excellent students, with Hugh also becoming a skilled horseman. Elizabeth is now four, and Anne two, with both girls doted on continuously by their brothers. Mary Ann has also passed halfway through another pregnancy, hoping that we will add another strong child to our home at the end of winter. The halls of this grand abode, which have echoed with the laughter and footsteps of my children during its construction, now sing with a life fully realized. It is a moment of personal triumph, a culmination of years of toil.

The presence of newspaper reporters on this day brought with it a flurry of interest and curiosity, their quill pens and pencils poised to document the grandeur. They marvelled at the edifice before them and remarked on its elegance. Their questions regarding the cost, a sum I openly declared to be ten thousand pounds, were followed with a tour of the luxury and finery that adorn each room. The domed ballroom, in the shape of a St Andrew's cross, is a clear statement that nothing is too grand for my family nor for the hundreds that will visit from Port Jackson and abroad to dine and dance with me here and partake in its pleasures.

As we traversed the villa, I watched their eyes widen with admiration at the fittings and furnishings, each piece of my and Mary Ann's choosing, ensuring that the residence was nothing short of enchanting. The reporters seemed utterly captivated by the gardens, a horticultural marvel set upon a hill that boasts a bounty of the finest fruits the climate can yield. The grounds, laid out with the utmost taste and care, were a particular source of awe, with their burgeoning orange trees and botanical rarities that rival the most esteemed gardens.

Their intrigue peaked as I spoke of the road, constructed through the bush at considerable expense, to provide a direct and genteel approach to our home. They had come via the private wharf and so knew it well. It was not only a stylish way for our guests to arrive but also provided alternate access in case of unforeseen occurrences on the road. My ship was berthed beside the wharf, well-used for tours of visiting dignitaries.

Of course, my band was a vital source of entertainment for all the visitors to this grand opening. It brings me great joy to be able to have them play each night under the veranda and provide their remarkable talents to events across the colony. Nothing stirs my heart like hearing the Highland piper play, and I ensure there is always one at the ready to meet my guests as they arrive on the barge. I am privileged in my position of harbour master that I may pluck the best musical talent from the convict boats, and other nobles across the colony are suitably jealous of my ability to provide these musicians with a good life at Henrietta Villa.

Some reporters questioned the large number of convict workers on the estate, now almost one hundred. However, I assured them these were all necessary to maintain such a stately home. It could not run without gardeners, domestic servants, footmen, and coachmen, and all were treated with due diligence and respect.

In our discourse, the topics of my friendship with the esteemed Macquarie and my role as a magistrate arose. To these inquiries, I responded with a sense of gravity and honour, expressing my earnest desire to fulfil these roles with integrity and to serve justice in all my capacities.

As our interview drew to a close, the reporters of the Gazette posed a question that caught me by surprise. They asked if I knew the title that whispers around the colony had bestowed upon me – The Prince of Australia. Hearing such a moniker attached to my person, I could not help but feel a mix of humour, humility and quiet pride. With all the sincerity of my being, I assured them that I am but a common man honoured to serve and that any title or accolade is a reflection of the love and duty I bear for this land and its people.

Thus, as I sit now in the embrace of Henrietta Villa, surrounded by the manifestations of my life's work, I cannot help but feel a profound gratitude. I thank the Lord for the bounty that he has seen fit to provide for my family despite my failings. And I pray our lives at Henrietta Villa continue always to be as fruitful and joyous. I also laugh at the thought of myself as the Prince of Australia. How far I have come from the Inn at Maybole. Still, I can hear my mother now warning me of how pride comes before a fall.

Henrietta Villa

TO THE HEART OF THE MAN

24 April 1822

In the serenity of my study, with the window ajar to the chorus of the morning, I sit to inscribe the events of this day, which has seen my name grace the pages of the Gazette. While flattering, the article scarcely does justice to the grandeur of Henrietta Villa, nor does it adequately preview the opulent entertainments, including truly beautiful balls, that have only begun to animate its halls. I muse upon this newfound title, 'Prince of Australia,' bestowed upon me and now published for the entire colony to see. I wonder if even the Prince of Wales, the intended recipient of our native kangaroo, has dined as lavishly or addressed as many illustrious gatherings as I now find routine.

The extent of my lands has grown vast, surpassing the estates of many others. With the recent acquisition of the Retreat at Vaucluse, my holdings now boast one acre in George Street, 190 acres at Point Eliza, an expanse of 475 acres at Vaucluse, the sweeping 1,130 acres at Woollahra, the fertile 295 acres at Petersham on the Parramatta Road, the strategic 80 acres at Botany Bay, a town allotment at Liverpool, two farms at Bringelly, 640 acres at Stony Creek, 300 acres in Van Diemen's Land, 2,000 acres in Bathurst, and the serene 200 acres at Neutral Bay. This portfolio secures not just my future but that of my children, and for this providence, my gratitude to the Almighty is boundless. Looking at this momentous list of assets, I would consider myself more of a king than a prince, but I best not tempt fate.

For with affluence comes the air of discontent. There are murmurings from some quarters who question the means I have used to amass my wealth and who harshly criticise Mary Ann's penchant for the latest French fashions. They seek to disparage our dignity and challenge our commitment to equality. But let it be known that our doors are open to all, regardless of birth or station. Mary Ann and I have pledged our resources to the noble cause of eroding the entrenched barriers of class. We do not judge or choose our company by the lineage of their blood but by the content of their character.

To affirm this commitment, I have embraced the Coat of Arms of my cousin, the son of my dear Uncle John and a man whose virtues have been recognised with a knighthood. The cry of "Feroci Fortier," bravery and strength, adopted by my distant relative, is now a statement that resonates with my deepest convictions. It shall be the maxim by which I lead my life, the call that will guide my actions. With this motto as my shield, I shall endeavour to live bravely, battle with courage, and uphold the Christian virtues that are the bedrock of our society.

I do understand how, for some, my confidence may be confused with pride. But I do not seek to boast, simply recognise that my achievements are born from the capabilities I have worked hard to develop and the responsibilities that I have successfully shouldered. I have a spirit that is both fierce and strong, and I am not sorry for where I stand. Let it be said that the Piper family, under the banner of "Feroci Fortier," will be champions of progress and pillars of charity for our cherished colony.

The Domed Ballroom at Henrietta Villa

19 March 1825

The nineteenth day of March, in the year of our Lord eighteen hundred and twenty-five, will be marked in history as one of jubilant festivity and unparalleled sport. I chose the occasion of St. Patrick's Day to bring my racetrack to life, and I have done so with such pomp and spectacle that it shall be remembered for years to come and no doubt will be etched within the annals of Sydney's history.

I had been planning this event for over a year, eager to celebrate the Irish culture and my growing stable, full of fine horses. The Irish have been downtrodden here for so long, enduring excessive treatment at the hands of many tyrants. I thought it the least I could do to put on an event to pay tribute to the patron saint of the Emerald Isle. The festivities were of a grandeur that even Sydney had not seen before, and yet, the fields were full of all manner of people, the highest of the high to the lowest of the low. Seeing this mix of fortunes and the camaraderie at each level of the community, my chest swelled with pride for the event I had masterminded.

From well before noon, a cavalcade of every vehicle imaginable gathered, a moving pageant towards the field of honour. The throngs agreed; there was no better place for such revelry than the grounds I had so carefully selected and cultivated for the very purpose of equestrian excellence. My participation was met with eager anticipation, and I rode with fervour but also fun. My trusted mare Gipsy bore me to a proud third, while Jessy, with her nimble grace, carried us to fifth. And on Everlasting, a noble beast, we secured yet another place of honour.

Amid this grandeur and gaiety were my seven children, with the laughter of William Sloper, now an active three-year-old and the coos of seven-month-old Alexander Septimus, wrapping us in joy. Hugh, now twelve, is an avid horse racer and seeks to pursue this as a possible career. I am endeared with his love of horses and hope that he may become a breeder, bringing all the care to his own stable that he has seen me endow upon mine. My wife and daughters, clad in the finest French fabrics, were the very image of beauty. At the same time, my sons, under Mary Ann's watchful eye, presented a visage of refinement and style. No one now looking at Mary Ann can disparage her for her convict heritage, for she is the epitome of God's grace.

Amidst the racing, the air was filled with music, the strains of which lifted the spirits and graced the intervals with merriment. A Highland Piper, in full regalia, commenced the event with a sonorous call that set hearts alight and concluded it with a melody that sang of memories of the old country, a fitting tribute to the noble tradition.

The race that shall be most recounted was that between the two greys - the Sheriff's formidable mare and my own spirited pony. At the starter's call, we dashed forth, a spectacle that captured every eye. The assembly erupted when the pony took a fright, pouncing forward and unseating me; my tumble was met with a thunderous hullabaloo from all sections of the crowd. Yet, in that moment of jest and jolt, my spirits remained unbroken, and I found a moment of great sportsmanship with the Sheriff, thus securing his favour and the respect of all who bore witness.

The day wound to a close with a display as varied as life itself. After the final race, there was a fleet of vehicles from the track that spanned the gamut of society, from the affluent to the modest. The road teemed with a jubilant parade, a throng of festivity that made passage a delightful challenge. The laden carts, overflowing with spirited attendees, sped homeward at a gallop that defied the usual tranquillity of the toll-gate road.

Not even the menacing presence of 'The Strippers' gang could curb the fanfare and celebration. Regardless, I have increased the security around all of our abodes and during our transportation, as the safety of my family is paramount.

We had a number of esteemed friends join us back at the Villa to continue the revelries. Dancing began after dinner, pausing only for supper at midnight and continuing until we all went to the lawns to watch the sunrise. I feel so very proud now in my ability now to bring so much joy to so many.

But for now, I must bathe my weary body and attend to my many bruises.

ST. PATRICK's DAY, AND THE RACES.

Last Thursday was ushered in with the usual testimonies of distinguished regard. Music struck up at an early hour, through our streets, to arouse the attention of the real Hibernian, upon the fourteen hundred and forty-second anniversary of his Patron Saint. In the forenoon every carriage, chariot, carricle, gig, horse, and cart, was in requisition to attend the races. The new course merits our entire approbation, as we think it one of the most elegible spots in the vicinity of Sydney, if four miles distance can be so termed; being below that facinating prospect of "Belle-vue." Subjoined we publish an account of the day's sports, which were handsomely forwarded us by one of our most worthy Correspondents. The afternoon, upon the conclusion of the ceremonies, exhibited a very interesting and grotesque display of the rich and poor, the high and the low, the small and the great. From the race-course to the South-head toll-gate, a distance of three miles, it was almost impossible to pass for road towards South-head for the excessively thronged multitude that were riding, driving, walking, singing, roaring, and racing their way homewards. Fortunately no accidents happened, though innumerable carts were heavily laden with passengers, and going at full gallop "up hill and down dale."

FIRST RACE....The following Horses started for a Subscription of One Hundred Dollars; the best of three heats; viz

Mr. Nash's horse, *Hector*, (rider thrown);
Mr. James Wright's bay mare, *Kitty*;
Mr. Taraner's mare, *Young Kitty*;
Mr. John Piper's favorite black mare, *Gipsy*;
Mr. James Badgery's horse, *Hector*;
Mr. Edward Frank's grey horse, *Captain*..-(Won by Mr. James Wright's bay mare, *Kitty*).

SECOND RACE, FOR SIXTY DOLLARS.

Mr. James Badgery's horse, *Hector*;
Mr. Nash's horse, *Hector*;
Mr. Kleusendorfie's horse, *Captain*;
Mr. R. Cooper's horse, *Wildman* (bolted);
Captain Piper's mare, *Jessy*;
Mr. Hill's mare, *My Lady*,--(Won by Mr. J. Badgery's bay horse, *Hector*.

THIRD RACE FOR A SADDLE AND BRIDLE.

Mr. Cooper's horse, *Wildman*;
Mr. Cowel's horse, *Swift*;
Captain Piper's horse, *Everlasting*;
Mr Taraner's mare, *Kitty*;
Mr. James White's mare, *Star*;
Mr. Solomon's mare, *Kitty*;
Mr. Wilford's horse, *Scratch*;
Mr. J. Nichols's mare, *Kitty*;
Captain Raine's mare, *Sprightly*.--(Won by Mr. Taraner's mare, *Kitty*.

Also, a Race between the Sheriff's grey horse, and Captain Piper's grey pony....Won by the former; the other having bolted, and throws her rider.

A second Race between Mr. Cullen's horse and Mr. ...

The dress of jockeys in 1825

30 July 1825

This day, I meet my diary with a heart wrenched asunder and my body wracked with the pain of grief. My dear boy. My darling boy, Hugh, is gone. Last week, we laid him to rest, and here I am, a mere shell of the man who was his father. Hugh was a mere twelve winters into his journey of life and so full of spirit. That is why he loved horses, for he shared their souls. He was racing his pony, only recently brought into the saddle when he was thrown. The image of his fall, his trampling beneath the relentless hooves of the pony, his body being thrashed around in the dirt, and the life leaving him is a vision that haunts my every waking hour and darkens my dreams. The knowledge that I was not there to hold him and tell him that he was dearly loved is like an endless torture.

My wife, Mary Ann, once a pillar of strength, now traverses the corridors of our home as a spectre of sorrow. She has lost her very essence, consumed by the void that Hugh has left. At moments, she seems to awake, and her anguish manifests in a tempest of rage. Her gaze pierces me with a fury born of despair. I stand accused, a silent defendant to her charge that my encouragement has wrought this tragedy upon us. I am, in her eyes, to blame for Hugh's love of horses and of racing, and I was the demon that led him into danger. I can find no energy to protest, for there is a partial truth in her indictments.

The echo of our son's laughter, once the very heartbeat of Henrietta Villa, has faded into silence so profound it roars in my ears and rips apart my soul. John, Thomas, Elizabeth, and Anne are swallowed by the shadow of mourning, their spirits fractured by their brother's absence. Though the girls try to cling to their mother, there is no comfort in her numb arms. Our youngest, Alexander and William, mirror our grief with innocent tears, sensing the chasm of loss that has sundered our family. Our dear friends have gathered around us, providing constant comfort and company to our family. I know their hands are on my back, and I hear them speak words of sympathy, but it is a scene that feels somehow separated from me.

Mary Ann has made the command, wrought from the depths of her torment, that Hugh's pony must be struck down by my own hand. This retribution, while understandable, I find truly reprehensible. To extinguish another life in the wake of such loss seems an act too cruel to bear, and I cannot bring myself to do it. She tells me that I have forsaken her. Still, I know in my heart that there is already far too much for the Lord to forgive me for, and taking another of his creatures would have me unrecognisable to myself and pushed well past the point of redemption.

Amidst this personal crisis, the tides of change do not cease. Governor Brisbane, whose support has been invaluable in my life, is departing. I am unsure how much more despair I can take before I, too, collapse. How am I to gather the shards of my broken spirit to present a respectable visage to the new administrator, Governor Darling?

Today, I am a man bereft, a father who has outlived yet another son. I pray for the strength to continue, to find a path through this darkest of nights, and to be a source of support for my family. Yet, in the quiet moments when the world retreats and I am left alone with my thoughts, the truth whispers with the cold clarity of a winter's breeze: all I long for is to join my son, to escape the unendurable pain of his absence.

TO THE HEART OF THE MAN

20 April 1826

On this day, I mark the passage of my fifty-third year, not with the sense of freedom of years past but with a heart burdened by distress. Henrietta Villa, once a symbol of my success is now the place where our friends and supporters gathered to prevent my disgrace.

Today, the Villa was alive with the sounds of celebration — a band played with vigour, the notes rising high above the laughter of guests. Fine food and wine graced every table, and the air was perfumed with a rich medley of aromas. Guests arrived by the barge-full, greeted by the haunting melodies of our Highland Piper. But beneath the merriment lurked a purpose most grave. This event was not merely a party but a gathering of support, a call for aid to stave off the potential loss of our home and honour.

My beloved Mary Ann, heavy with the promise of new life, carries her burden with beauty. Still, she has not regained the lustre she had before the loss of Hugh. She showed our guests a face of gaiety, but in the quiet times in front of the hearth, her fragility and fear are forthcoming. Hugh's loss still lingers close by, and we both are gravely worried lest anything happens to the child in her womb. The veneer over our wound is still tenuously thin, and any misfortune might fracture it.

Governor Darling, a man who was the subject of whispered warnings, has proven to be the harbinger of my undoing. Under Macquarie, I found a friend. Under Darling, I have met my nemesis. His arrival was swift, his intentions clear — to purge the colony of those he deemed to have profited unduly. With merciless efficiency, his investigators descended upon us, tearing through the records of the Naval Office. My systems were declared deficient, and my attention to duty was publicly questioned. The swift abolition of the Naval Office and my subsequent demotion to Comptroller of Customs — these were but the first slashes of Darling's incisive blade, but they have cut me deeply and threaten to bleed me dry.

The Governor's stratagems to break my spirit did not end there. He introduced the requirement for all customs payments to be made immediately and deemed me personally liable for their delivery. There were not yet sufficient funds in the coffers to cover the rates he had set, so now I have been forced to draw from personal savings to cover the shortfall. Only the mortgaging of my beloved Villa prevented the disgrace of default. If I lose my position though, there will not be sufficient income to maintain the Villa into the future. Thus, the gathering, veiled in the trappings of a birthday fete, was, in truth, a plea for the preservation of our home. Loyal friends arrived with open hearts and generous hands.

Yet, even as I offer thanks for their support, I am acutely aware that their kindness cannot mend the tarnish on my reputation, now seriously sullied by Darling's relentless campaign. The raid on the offices of the Bank of New South

Wales, where I preside as Chairman, laid bare a loan that exposed us to substantial creditor risk. I admitted honestly to knowing the borrowers and that the loans were granted at my behest. But no one continued listening to hear that the creditors were men of honour and would have fulfilled their obligations as and when required. Darling seized upon this situation to cast doubt over the sturdiness of my stewardship and to suggest that I had used my station purely for personal benefit. He declared that I had caused great detriment to the bank and all those who had trusted it with their money. I tendered my resignation with a heavy heart, shouldering the blame to shield my fellow directors from what was, in reality, a shared shame.

Governor Darling, whose background as a military man has given him a taste for order and discipline, has wielded his power with a precision that has left little room for redemption. His intention to reform the colony's administration, to cleanse it of perceived excesses and inefficiencies, has been a double-edged sword that now points at my legacy. I remember my conversations in London with Macarthur when he, too, was at the precipice of poverty. At that time, I felt superior, considering him brash and excessive. It appears now that I have faltered in heeding my own advice. I now see that Macarthur has been restored to his former glory, establishing the Australian Agricultural Company, a corporation that serves to bolster his profits handsomely. He has also been welcomed back to the corridors of power, being placed in the New South Wales Legislative Assembly. The winds of fortune are certainly fickle. I pray that they turn back in our favour soon. Elizabeth has been a solid source of advice and care during this most difficult time, but even she cannot stop this storm.

As the last of the lamps are extinguished on this day of false revelry, I find myself reflecting on the future of my family. What shall become of us as the favour I once held fades? What shall become of our children as their futures are tainted by scandal? The laughter of our guests could not mask the fear that claws at my soul — the fear of an uncertain future where the hard-earned assets of a lifetime may be reduced to mere memories.

In the solitude of my study, I pray for the strength to stand through this weather and to reclaim some semblance of respect. May the Lord watch over us, and may the generosity of our friends be the guiding light that leads us back to safer shores.

15 August 1826

In the quiet solitude of this early morning, I sit with a soul consumed by darkness. In His inscrutable wisdom, the Lord has seen fit to call another of my children home. My son, Frederick, a tender soul of only three months, has been excised from our embrace. Each son's departure carves a deeper wound, and this latest loss brings with it a pain as fresh and raw as the first.

The weight of this grief is a burden almost too formidable to bear, and yet, at the same time, I must also manage Governor Darling's relentless pursuit of my pride. He continues to uncover failings in my past service at the Naval Office and to scrutinise my dealings at the bank with a predatory zeal. His focused attention feels like a noose tightening around my neck. He is resolute in his campaign to see me fall, and I have no means to defend my honour.

Mary Ann, my dear wife, is herself drowning in grief, her despair manifesting as a relentless drive for me to act, to do something — anything — to cling to the prosperity we are on the brink of losing. Her pain, raw and unyielding, turns towards me, seeking a target for the anguish that consumes her. I stand at the centre of this maelstrom, pulled by the currents of Darling's vendetta and Mary Ann's anguish, feeling trapped, useless, and utterly devoid of worth.

As I am plunged into the depths of depression, I cling to a singular duty; to protect my family. This is the only footing I can find in this enveloping darkness. Yet, as I struggle to find the path that will restore our honour, a sinister thought whispers, questioning the point of this unending struggle. Surely, there must be a point when it becomes sensible to submit to an inexorable tide.

With each passing day, the energy to continue this fight wanes, and the whispers become louder, leaving behind a hollow shell of a man who once held dreams of legacy. The thought of surrender, once inconceivable, now lingers at the edge of my consciousness, a seductive siren promising an end to this torment.

I must find the strength to continue, not for myself, but for the family that depends on me. Yet, in the darkest hours of the night, when the world sleeps, and I am alone with my torment, I confess that I am besieged by thoughts most foul — the contemplation of a final, desperate escape from the agony that is my existence.

Lord, hear my plea; grant me a sign, a sliver of hope, a reason to endure. For now, I am but a weary traveller at the crossroads, my will to journey forth nearly extinguished.

Mary Ann Piper with four of her fourteen children.

TO THE HEART OF THE MAN

4 March 1827

Today marks the day I have resolved upon a course most grave, a decision borne not of impulse but of a deep and abiding despair. I have concluded that my time in this world must come to an end. The prospect of witnessing my fifty-fourth year has become impossible, for the burden of shame I have ushered upon my family weighs too heavily upon my soul.

The news of my son Norfolk's passing last month at the tender age of eighteen has added another layer to the already insurmountable grief. It is one that I cannot share with Mary Ann, for she will not hear naught about a child that brings her embarrassment. The spectre of death seems to linger with a morbid fascination over my lineage, claiming my children with a cruel and relentless hand. And so, I have decided to offer my own life, hoping that those remaining may be spared.

Governor Darling is going further in his unyielding harassment of me and my honour. He has stripped me of all public duties and uncovered a deficiency at the bank that looms large as a dark cloud over my head — a sum of twelve thousand pounds for which I am held accountable. He has assured the public that I am absolved of the charge of theft, yet has made it clear that my actions equated to gross mismanagement, an accusation that casts me down with the weight of an anchor.

With no means to settle this gargantuan debt, I am now falling over the precipice of ruin. The generosity of friends has been expended in the upkeep of Henrietta Villa, leaving only a pittance for emergencies. Even if money were to fall from the heavens into Henrietta Villa, it would do little to repair my reputation among those who will decide my future employment. This man has been my undoing, and now I only hope he will be happy with my death.

Thus, I am cornered, and there is but one path left to tread. This resolution has haunted my thoughts. But after tonight I will be free of all worry.

I have set my affairs in order, penning a new will and composing my final missives. This evening, I shall break bread with those dearest to me, a final gathering shrouded in the guise of fellowship. None of them will know the true nature of this supper. I do not create a crowd for my own benefit but to ensure there is sufficient support for Mary Ann and the children. For they will need many loving arms around them. They will no longer have mine.

I harbour no illusions of martyrdom; I am no saviour. Rather, I am the architect of my own damnation, destined, I fear, for the fiery depths. The plan is set: Aboard the barge, under the cloak of night, I will commit my spirit to the depths, a final surrender to the waters that brought me here.

In this act, I seek not valour but escape from a crisis from which there is no redemption. Mary Ann, my beloved, and our children shall be liberated from the chains of my failures, free to forge a path unburdened by the legacy of a man who brought naught but hardship and sorrow.

I depart this world leaving behind a family whose love I was unworthy of, children and grandchildren who will bear the stain of my actions. Yet, in this final act, I cling to the belief that it manifests a true man's will — to shield those he loves from further pain by removing the source of their suffering.

As I stand on the brink of eternity, my soul is wracked with doubt and fear, yet resolute in the belief that there is no other way. May God have mercy on me, for I can find none for myself.

The view towards Henrietta Villa.

4 June 1827

Today, I am a man undone, not dead in body, but in the mind of Sydney's society, forced into the dim recesses of humiliation and dishonour. My once proud estate, Henrietta Villa, is being dismantled piece by piece, its contents laid bare for the vultures to pick over. I cannot, will not, bear witness to this spectacle, to the eager hands rifling through the remnants of my life, their greedy eyes measuring my downfall in pounds and pence.

I thought I had found the very bottom of my shame that fateful night upon the barge when I hoped to sink to the bottom and be done with this life. Yet, here I stand, submerged further still in the mire of my own making. The irony of my failed escape from this mortal coil is not lost on me; it has only served to deepen the hate I feel for myself and those who would now seek to benefit from my failure. I have hidden the Coat of Arms calling "Feroci Fortier", knowing full well that if it was found, it would only be used as further evidence of the farce I have become.

The crew on the barge, bless their loyal hearts, did not see the final act of a desperate man but a mishap, a mistaken fall. Their swift intervention, pulling my limp form from the embrace of the cold, indifferent waters, was an act of salvation I neither desired nor deserved. To awaken to the mixed gaze of relief and scorn in Mary Ann's eyes was a torment of its own kind. Her anger has been constant since that night and speaks loudly of betrayal, of a trust irrevocably broken.

Yet, she remains bound, I believe, not by love but by necessity and the stark reality that a woman of her standing, especially one encumbered with children, faces bleak prospects alone. My attempted departure from this life has cemented my legacy, not as a man of honour but as a coward, a devil towards those who depended on me most.

As the sale of Henrietta Villa proceeds without my presence, I am beset by a bitter realisation. Those who come, drawn by the prospect of bargains, find joy in my despair. Each item sold, each cherished memory auctioned off for a fraction of its worth, is further confirmation of my failure. They do not see the pieces of a life once lived; they see opportunities to enrich themselves at the expense of my downfall.

The mockery that permeates the air is a poison I refuse to breathe. I am a pariah in my own land, a cautionary tale of ambition and hubris laid low. Once spoken with a measure of respect, my name is now uttered with disdain, a byword for disgrace and dereliction of duty.

The sale of Henrietta Villa marked the dissolution of my dreams and the grim reality that I could no longer afford to pay my loyal servants. This failure weighs heavily on my conscience as I grapple with the guilt of letting down those who depended on me most, fearing deeply for their future in a world I can no longer shield them from.

In the wake of this public humiliation, I find myself grappling with an anger that consumes me. I am angry at those who delight in my misfortune, at a fate that has left me bereft of dignity, and at myself for the choices that have led me here to be in hiding. I will not harbour hate for the Lord, for his teachings forewarned this future. It was I who did not listen.

So, we will pack up all we own here and leave for Bathurst. Our property there, a largely unknown territory, and all that we have left, will be our place of retreat. The only sweetness I can find is in the generous embraces of my angels, my daughters, Elizabeth and Anne.

TO THE HEART OF THE MAN

16 July 1827

The pall of grief that has enveloped me since the passing of D'Arcy Wentworth has been dark and unyielding. His departure from this world has left a void in my heart, one that today's events have only served to deepen. This morning, as I sat amidst the congregation, I found myself the reluctant recipient of a sermon by Samuel Marsden, a figure whose notoriety for severity precedes him. From his elevated position at the pulpit, Marsden's gaze seemed to single me out, a silent accusation before the words even left his lips.

D'Arcy's life was one founded on liberal values. He was a true champion for a just and equitable society, a stark contrast to the oppressive doctrines Marsden espouses. The titles Marsden bears of "the flogging parson" and "the hanging judge" are not unwarranted. He has a penchant for cruelty, which he hides under the guise of his divine mandate. Today, however, his sermon struck a chord, not for its spiritual guidance but for its thinly veiled personal attack. With a pointedness that left little doubt of his target, Marsden recited a verse from Timothy: "Those who want to get rich fall into temptation and are caught in the trap of many foolish and harmful desires, which pull them down to ruin and destruction."

The hypocrisy of Marsden's message was not lost on me. Here was a man who, while preaching the perils of materialism and the spiritual bankruptcy it entails, indulges in the very pursuits he condemns. Marsden's own fervent accumulation of wealth, his zeal for securing riches at every turn, stands in stark contrast to the cautionary tale he cast upon me from the pulpit. The irony of receiving such counsel from one so embroiled in the quest for material gain is a bitter irony indeed.

Yet, even as I grapple with this mixture of grief and indignation, I am compelled to consider my own path. Marsden's use of scripture to chastise those ensnared by the lure of wealth prompts a moment of introspection. Amidst the sorrow of Wentworth's passing and the sting of Marsden's critique, I find myself questioning the legacy I wish to leave behind.

And while I am still navigating the shame of loss and public censure, I do not want Wentworth's vision to become undone. He was a true inspiration, and I was honoured to call him my friend. I owe him much, and so I will not let myself crumple under the evil eye of Marsden. I will pick myself up and work towards what Wentworth was aiming for. I will be guided by his dream of a community founded on compassion, justice, and the kind of prosperity that enriches the soul rather than corrupts it.

Marsden may have metered out a harsh lesson, but I will not give him the satisfaction of seeing me fall further. I am resolved to honour my friend's memory by striving for a society that reflects the best of our human capacities. In the face of hypocrisy and condemnation, I hold fast to the belief that true worth lies not in the accumulation of wealth but in the legacy of kindness and equity we build for future generations. I can no longer give my children material possessions, but I can give them even more precious gifts. With God and Wentworth as my witnesses, this is what I will do.

TO THE HEART OF THE MAN

30 November 1827

As I pen this entry, the air of Bathurst carries with it the heat of late November but also another blessing. Today, our family welcomed Mary Adrewina into the world, a symbol of our new beginnings here in Bathurst. Her arrival fills me with great hope, tempered only by concern for her fragility and how one so tiny may fare in the fierce heat that is yet to come. I pray for her health and that I may make a comfortable future for all in this place.

I am heartened to think that we now make our home in place named after the man who first believed in my abilities, Lord Bathurst. I see it as a sign that here we shall receive the same support this great man has shown me.

However, our journey here was nothing short of an odyssey, fraught with the perils of crossing the Blue Mountains. The path, a winding serpent through rugged terrain, held the constant threat of bushranger attacks and confrontations with the native people. The expedition required unwavering vigilance and an iron resolve, particularly as we navigated the treacherous river crossings. Each wagon, laden with the remnants of our Sydney life — including, controversially, one of Henrietta Villa's brass cannons — had to be painstakingly unloaded, ferried across by punt, and reloaded to resume the journey by road. Despite the murmurs of disapproval from onlookers, we were determined to transplant a piece of our former elegance to our new surroundings, refusing to let adversity strip us of our dignity.

I have named our new home here in Bathurst "Alloway Bank" in memory of a village I hold dear from my homeland. I hope it too, like the Alloway I know in Scotland, shall be a place of peace.

Settling in has been a venture into both the familiar and the unknown. The house itself, though modest compared to the grandeur of Henrietta Villa, has been adorned with the fine possessions that survived our departure from Sydney and which provide some sense of consistency.

However, the weather here is markedly different from the coastal climes we're accustomed to. The intense heat of late November, absent the mitigating sea breeze, makes some days simply deflating. Mary Ann finds it particularly uncomfortable, requiring regular repose to recover her congenial countenance. Yet, within this challenge lies opportunity — the chance to forge a new legacy far from the malicious whispers of Sydney society.

I find myself invigorated by the prospect of creating something from the land. The community's lack of cheese presents an opportunity for innovation and entrepreneurship. I am set on mastering the art of cheese-making, envisioning it as the cornerstone of a flourishing enterprise that will bring both pleasure and prosperity to our new home. The work to

226

deliver such an endeavour is arduous. Still, despite the heat and the hardship, I believe the labour will lead to a full life for my family.

The children have adapted with an admirable blend of excitement and resilience. While daunting, the journey's ordeal has imbued them with a sense of adventure and unity that will shape their characters for the better. I had forgotten the joys of sitting around a simple campfire by night and navigating by the sun and the stars. It was such a joy to share this with the children, although there were times when the youngest were scared by the darkness and the vast sense of space and snuggled safely within my arms. John Junior, in particular, has shown commendable fortitude, and his assistance was invaluable throughout our trek. He impressed me with his patience, his physical strength, but also the care he showed to all of the crew. I am truly blessed to have him as my boy.

Alloway Bank, with its budding gardens and flourishing fields, holds so much hope. As we acclimate to the rhythms of rural life, I am reminded of the power of perseverance, the value of family, and the endless potential of the land. Here, in Bathurst, we will lay the foundations for a lasting legacy, one far greater than any fortune man can bestow. Here, we can have the space and time to be with our children, to watch them grow and build a community that God would be proud of.

TO THE HEART OF THE MAN

The Piper wagons crossing the Blue Mountains.

CAPTAIN PIPER, the promoter of harmony and good fellowship wherever he goes, is at last firmly fixed on his estate at Bathurst. His bugles, which accompanied the last wagon of furniture, struck up as they were passing the Blue Mountains, the lively tune of "Over the hills and far away," to the great delight of the drivers of all the carts and drays they met with on the road. ~ The Monitor, 4 October 1827

Alloway Bank in Bathurst

4 October 1829

The aura of Alloway Bank was one of palpable anticipation and excitement as we prepared to host Governor Darling, an event that has cemented our place in the Bathurst community and is a clear display of our social resilience. As the day dawned, the household was a flurry of activity, with every servant and family member contributing to the seamless execution of the evening's festivities. I prided myself on the lack of animosity, the air of gentility that I provided to Governor Darling, mending over the maliciousness of the past. In fact, I send praises and thanks to the Lord for this chance to show him some generosity and compassion. However, I hope the Lord will forgive me for choosing not to sound the cannon at his arrival. I trust the day's events more than compensated for its absence.

John Junior, now a man at twenty-one, took the lead in showing Governor Darling around our estate, his pride in our operations evident as he detailed the intricacies of our ever-expanding cheese venture, the efficiency of our coach houses and stables, and the productivity of our dairy and blacksmith shop. His demonstration of competence and vision left me swelling with pride. I daresay it also impressed upon the Governor the potential within my son and now Alloway Bank's manager. I think, too, he saw the graciousness of all of my children; Thomas, thirteen; Elizabeth, eleven; Anne, nine;

William, seven; Alexander, five; Mary, two; and our newborn daughter, Phyllis. Perhaps now, after spending time with me and my family, he may consider his cruelty misguided. Hopefully he can see the honour and humility that I seek to bring to all of my endeavours. However, if he leaves with no better perception of the Piper clan, at least he will depart well entertained.

The evening's gathering was a lavish affair designed to showcase the best of Alloway Bank and introduce the Governor to the warmth and hospitality for which we wish to be known. The dining table groaned under the weight of the sumptuous fare, reflective of the richness available in Bathurst. Dishes comprised of locally sourced meats, including succulent lamb and beef, complemented by an array of vegetables from our gardens. However, our cheese became the centrepiece of the meal, and each variety was very well received. Governor Darling's generous praise of our produce filled me with hope. It ignited a vision of expanding our distribution to the nobility in Sydney. With the Governor's referral, this is a goal now firmly within our sights.

The displays and dances that followed dinner were a lively showcase of the cultural blend that Bathurst has become. Traditional reels and jigs filled the air, accompanied by the harmonious blend of violin and flute, inviting everyone into a spirited participation that blurred the lines between status and rank. It was in these moments of shared joy and revelry that Alloway Bank truly shone, embodying the spirit of community and, finally, the potential for unity under Governor Darling's administration.

During his visit, Governor Darling was also taken on a tour of Bathurst, allowing him to look at the landmarks that define our colony and the evidence of our many challenges. From the breathtaking views of the Macquarie River, which sustains our lands and livelihoods, to the town centre that pulses with the promise of growth, he saw the heart of our community. Yet, it was in our discussions of the issues plaguing Bathurst — land disputes, the need for infrastructure development, and the ever-present threat of bushrangers — that I found the Governor most engaged. His insights and the assurances of support gave me hope that, under his guidance, Bathurst might overcome its hurdles and thrive.

As I retire to pen this entry, I am filled with a renewed sense of purpose and a belief in the bright future that lies ahead for us here. The success of our enterprise, the potential for increased prosperity, and the unity exhibited in our gathering give me much motivation to continue this mission, one in which we contribute to the greater good of Bathurst and its people.

TO THE HEART OF THE MAN

27 June 1831

Drought has come and deadened Bathurst. Our once lively fields are now parched expanses of despair. The land around Alloway Bank, typically abuzz with the vibrancy of life, now lies dormant under the oppressive heat. The soil, cracked and dry, no longer supports the lush pastures that fed our cows, causing a heart-wrenching halt to our cheese production. It pains me deeply to see the bounty of our land so diminished. The scant milk we manage to pull from the cows is now a lifeline, not for our business, but for the children in our community. The welfare of these young souls must take precedence over any thought of profit. I am sending my workers to our neighbours' houses with whatever milk we can spare to ensure they, too, will survive this torrid time.

Amid this adversity, two remarkable events have occurred that create much cause for happiness. The birth of my daughter, Jane Adelaide, two days prior has brought a burst of life into our lives. Unfortunately, duty called me away to Sydney, and I was absent for her arrival into this world. Yet, this absence was for a cause that marked an important turning point in my life - my reinstatement as a magistrate. This honour signifies a restoration of my reputation and a return to my roots, where I believe I can contribute most effectively to the common good. In Sydney, amidst the legal proceedings, I felt a profound sense of purpose, a reaffirmation of my commitment to justice and equity. I have lived in many lodgings over the course of my life, but it is within the walls of the courtroom that I feel I truly belong.

Whilst in Sydney, I had the pleasure of riding about the first paddle steamer and reading the first publication of the Sydney Morning Herald, which I am sure will become a vital source of information for the colony and beyond. The administration is preparing for an influx of emigrants, with the plan for these to drive expansion and reduce the reliance on convict labour. Over the next years, our shores will be flooded with settlers from all of the English Isles as well as China, America and Germany. In a few years, I suspect the colony I landed in many years ago will be unrecognisable with a menagerie of many cultures.

I know Mary Ann was worried about my time away. I could see the fear in her eyes as I said farewell. She knows full well about my frailties, and Sydney is awash with temptation. However, she need not be afraid. I am now a relatively old man and am no longer the attractive prospect I once was. More importantly, though, I am steadfast in my determination to not sin again. I do appreciate John seeing me off and asking me solemnly not to do anything in Sydney that would shame my mother. His words truly hurt, and yet I know they were born from great care and his growing wisdom about the wickedness that lies within man. He has helped to keep me honest and out of harm's way.

For now, as an outsider, I can see how easy it is to get caught up in the swirling storms of Sydney's politics and society. I am glad to return to Bathurst, to my simple home and pleasures. In Sydney, I felt like a leaf caught in a tempest. Now, back at Alloway Bank, this leaf has settled back into its rightful place.

With our land still gripped by drought, our Sundays have taken on a new routine, one that, despite the physical toll, has become a cherished ritual. The journey to Church is a four-mile trek, and our horses are too weak to walk it. So, we do it ourselves, and this saunter has become a time for family bonding. Dressed in our Sunday best, Mary Ann and I, along with our children, make the pilgrimage on foot. The children, in their neatly pressed dresses and suits, embody the resilience and style that Mary Ann brings to our family. The younger ones, often too weary to complete the journey on their own, find solace in our arms, their weight a reminder of the responsibilities we carry. These walks, though exhausting, are punctuated with laughter and learning. Upon reaching the Church, we welcome the opportunity to rest, to sit in contemplation and prayer, surrounded by our community, drawing comfort and courage for the days ahead.

After several years away from Sydney society, I find Mary Ann returned to the beautiful calm being I remember on Norfolk Island. She remarks that she has forgiven me for losing the riches we held and that she honestly prefers the simple joys that bind us as a family here in Bathurst. She admits that the incessant competition in the colony wearied her, whereas here, she feels her heart restored. While the revelries and luxuries were a source of inspiration and excitement, she tells me frequently that they cannot compare to the companionship she now feels within this community and the walls of this home. She feels more secure here than she ever could around stately homes, bustling streets and gossip sessions with the other wives. I thank the Lord, with all that I am, for delivering us to this place of peace.

25 May 1834

On this day, our household was enveloped in a joyous clamour, marking a departure from our usual solemn Sunday observances. My beloved Mary Ann was delivered of a son, whom we have named Henry, infusing our home with a new burst of happiness. Though modest in its celebration compared to the grandeur we accorded Governor Bourke, this felicitous event has nonetheless been a to share a toast or two with our trusted friends.

The townsfolk still murmur with amusement over the extravagant salute we gave Governor Bourke when he came to visit Bathurst. We decided to fire the cannon in his honour—a spectacle marred by the humorous mishap of the cannon's recoil, which saw it fling backwards and demolish a wall. True to their profession, the musicians played on, undeterred. This incident has etched our family more deeply into the annals of this community, and it is a tale regularly recounted with laughter. The youngest of our flock, though, may never get over their fear of cannons. The babies were shocked to tears, and the toddlers took flight to the safe confines of the house.

Despite the grip of a drought that has strained our resources and spirits, we presented Governor Bourke with a table laden with the finest provisions our estate and the surrounding land could muster. Local game, harvested crops that had defiantly weathered the dry season, and the last of our stored cheeses were arrayed with care and adorned with hand-crafted decorations.

The evening was illuminated by entertainment designed to capture the essence of our community. Local musicians, whose melodies have long been a source of comfort and revelry in our gatherings, played with a passion that seemed to lift the weight of concern from our shoulders. Recitations and dances, rooted in our homeland's traditions and this new land's evolving culture, unfolded under the stars. It was a night where the laughter and camaraderie momentarily eclipsed the dread of uncertainty that this dry spell brings. Dancing is a whirlwind of joy — a liberation of body and spirit. It was my greatest pleasure to share many a dance with my darling Mary Ann and my beautiful daughters, Elizabeth and Anne, who seem to enjoy the turns and twirls as much as I do.

Governor Bourke's journey into Bathurst was not merely a ceremonial visit but a pivotal moment for our town. Accompanied by influential figures, he toured our lands, witnessing firsthand the challenges we faced. Just like Governor Darling did five years prior, he held discussions with the town's leaders and delved into the pressing issues at hand. And similar to his predecessor, Governor Bourke listened attentively, offering words of encouragement and discussing potential measures to mitigate these hardships. He left us feeling that while there were no immediate fixes, our struggles had been acknowledged and that avenues for assistance might be forthcoming.

The successful visit by Governor Bourke also piqued the curiosity of Dr Lang, known both for his scathing critiques and his journalistic endeavours with the Colonist. He also came to stay at Alloway Bank and to examine where moral reform was required. Despite his stern views against societal vices and his aggressive attacks on the licentiousness he perceived in colonial society, he found in Alloway Bank an exemplar of virtue. His acknowledgment of our family's elegance, our devout gatherings for prayer, and the dignity of our household softened his usual rigour. It was clear to him that I was a man not just of resolute character and capability but of profound faith. He left having confirmed for himself and his readers that ours was not just another den of corruption, but a place of true Christian compassion.

There have been many highlights of my life thus far, with the recent establishment of a Scots Church in Bathurst a momentous one to add. It is a grand achievement for our Scottish community and bears witness to our enduring faith and respect for our heritage. This Church offers a sanctuary where we may practice our beliefs and honour those who came before us. My contribution to its realisation I gave in tribute to the Lord's support that has been constant throughout my trials and triumphs. I am deeply honoured to have advocated for its inception and rallied our flock to bring this to fruition. This Church will truly be recorded as one of my greatest achievements.

I am saddened to report that the pain of the past drought still lingers, yet recent rains have sparked a flicker of optimism. John Junior and I are eager to revive the dairy and cheese production, and we both pray that the rains continue regularly enough to make this a reality. There are days when John Junior is downcast and depressed, not dissimilar to so many other settlers who are struggling through the dry. I remind him gently that God takes care of the birds in the sky, and so He will also show us mercy. This has led to many heated and yet heartwarming conversations about what man wants and what he truly needs. John and I have some differing views but it is a delight to join him in the debate.

The month also brought some incredibly sombre news; John Macarthur is dead, and his passing has been felt deeply. Elizabeth had been estranged from him for some time, unable to live sensibly and safely with his increasing melancholy and unpredictable paranoia. She bore the trials of his insanity with admirable fortitude, and I do not doubt that Macarthur's death now comes with some sense of relief. Her resilience and wisdom have held her family together during this trying time, and I know shall continue to in the future. Though my duties in Bathurst prevented my attendance at the funeral, my thoughts and condolences have been fervently dispatched to Elizabeth, with hopes that she may find peace and perhaps, in time, join us in the warmth of Alloway Bank. Although I do not expect she will visit anytime soon, as she will be, as always, hard at work securing her husband's enterprises.

11 April 1843

As I near the threshold of my seventieth year, I am confronted with a reality I had desperately hoped to evade. Today, I have declared myself insolvent, a proclamation that carries with it a hefty weight of disappointment and despair. My son, John Junior, faces a similar fate. We have shared many successes at Alloway Bank, and now we also share this tribulation.

For the past six years, I have worked with every ounce of my being to revive the parched earth of Alloway Bank and to breathe life back into our farm. The first drought, a decade ago, tested our resolve but left us hopeful; through loans, we clung to our lifestyle, firmly believing the rains would return to restore our lands and our fortunes. But the second drought six years ago was far too close to the first. We had not had enough time to fully recover. It was this second battle that lay bare the fragility of our financial foundation. Despite my efforts as a magistrate, the income was insufficient to stem the tide of mounting debts. Our genteel façade crumbled, revealing the harsh truth of our imprudence and the unsustainable nature of our aspirations.

The process of itemising the assets of Alloway Bank for sale has been a harrowing one. Each entry in the ledger, each piece of land, livestock, and furniture marked for auction, feels like a piece of my soul being stripped away. I failed to foresee and forestall this dire outcome. In hindsight, the signs were there; some would say they were even screaming at me. Yet we were blinded by pride and an unwavering attachment to the status and comforts we had come to know. It is a painful acknowledgment that, had we lived more modestly and managed our resources with greater caution, we might not have found ourselves here in this humiliation once again.

For this declaration of insolvency is not merely a financial reckoning but a blow to my family's honour. The thought of relinquishing Alloway Bank, the heart of our family's life and labour, is a source of anguish I find difficult to bear. Uncertainty again looms large, as we still have not secured another suitable lodging, one which we can sustain financially.

Yet, I have been in such a place before, in fact, twice now. I dismantled the colony on Norfolk Island, removing lives and livelihoods, and while this was distressing, I survived to see a new day. The sale of Henrietta Villa and my prized possessions was also a time of great heartache and shame. Still, I stand here today amongst friends and family. This is but another harsh lesson that we live within a nature that is in constant flux. Yes, I fear for what may come next, and yet I also have faith. I have witnessed the Lord's providence delivered in our darkest hours, and as we prepare for the auction of Alloway Bank, I again seek His guidance.

15 October 1845

Sometimes, God does not speak through spirits or scriptures, but through the steadfast hands of firm friends. Such was the grace bestowed upon us by my dear friend William Wentworth. I called on him to release the remaining donations gathered from the sale of Henrietta Villa, and he delivered them promptly.

However, despite my passionate prayers, the sum, though generous, fell short of the debt that would secure our home. It was not sufficient to release Alloway Bank from insolvency. Yet, it bore the seeds of a new beginning in the form of a modest abode on Westbourne, where we have since taken refuge. This sanctuary, entrusted in Mary Ann's name by Wentworth's meticulous arrangement, promises a semblance of stability for her and our children, a gesture that inscribes his name forever in our hearts.

Stripped of assets and devoid of any standing in the eyes of financial arbiters, I find myself remarkably at peace. In this state of calm, I sometimes wonder whether I, too, am slipping into insanity. But the feelings are true; I have finally found wealth beyond measure. Our new life, marked by simplicity, offers abundant time for devotion, the nourishing solace of prayer, and the cherished company of my family. The joyous visits from our grown children, now with families of their own, infuse our home with laughter and warmth, a balm for Mary Ann's spirit and mine alike. I have been released from the multitude of worries that plagued me each moment when I oversaw both property and people. There is a price to pay for power, and it no longer exacts its toll on me here.

Jane, our beautiful and gracious daughter, has chosen a path of unwavering loyalty to our small circle, forsaking the prospect of marriage to remain by our side. She is such a generous, tender-hearted and wise girl, spending time with the aboriginals who wander through the property and learning more about this land than I ever could from scratching at its surface. The stories she shares offer comfort and curiosity. Her sweet piano playing brings me a sense of stillness that mere words cannot express how much I appreciate. As I traverse what is likely the winter of my years, I pray that I may be of little burden to her and that my final reckoning will be swift. I have found and rehung the Coat of Arms above my reading chair. The words "Feroci Fortier" are a much-needed reminder as I head towards my end.

I still recoil when I think of all the pain I have caused across my life and the losses that are now also a part of my legacy. However, I will no longer allow them to sink me into shame. With the Lord's strength, I place my hand on my heart and take responsibility for all I have done and not done and all for the consequences of my actions, both honourable and hurtful. There is so much I yearn to undo, lives I would like to restore, and interludes that I would like the chance once again to ignore. I do wish I had been there to prevent Hugh from racing on the pony, to have been more prudent with my power at the bank and to have remained ever faithful to Mary Ann. However, I do not know whether these things may have delivered any better outcome. Only the Lord knows what might have been.

I am ready to leave this Earth, not of my own hand as I had so selfishly tried before, but at the time and place that the Lord decrees. I turn my life over, not to my will, or even that of Mary Ann's, but to my Lord's. My earlier attempt at taking the reins of divine timing seems senseless. I surrender my fate not to mortal desires but to the will of the Lord. I am prepared to embrace whatever end He ordains. For this is true freedom.

The pursuit of fame and fortune, once the focus of my existence, has yielded little except for one profound realisation. Wealth is not found in what we own. It lies in the intangible currency of love and labour — in embraces, laughter, and sorrows shared, in the birthing of and caring for creations, and the simple, unadorned duties and dances of our days. These are the treasures I will carry forth, etched not in stone but in my soul. These are the lights that show the way to the heart of the man.

Westbourne House Bathurst

Captain John Piper (1774-1851)

TO THE HEART OF THE MAN

About the Author

Belinda Tobin is a researcher, author, producer, and avid explorer of the human experience, with all its challenges and complexities. Her works span fiction, non-fiction, poetry, tv series and film. However, they all share a common purpose, to foster a more conscious, compassionate, courageous and connected future.

Find out more about Belinda and her projects at www.belindatobin.com.

TO THE HEART OF THE MAN

For more titles go to:
www. heart-led.pub/bel-house-books